This paperback edition published in 2024

First published in Great Britain by Amazon

The moral right of the author has been asserted.

All rights reserved. Without limiting the rights under copyright reserved above, no part of this publication may be reproduced, stored or introduced into a retrieval system, or transmitted, in any form or by any means (electronic, mechanical, photocopying, recording or otherwise), without the prior written permission of both the copyright owner and the publisher of this book.

The characters and the events in this book are fictious. Any similarity to real persons, dead or alive, is coincidental and not intended by the author.

Copyright © 2024 Krystal Zammit

All rights reserved.

ISBN: 9798323112791

For my dad and mum, Vince and Julie, who bought me my first pen. And for Ralph whose name shall never be forgotten.

CONTENTS

	Acknowledgments	i
1	Paproć	1-12
2	Seasonal Skies	13-18
3	Pen & Paper	19-29
4	Download, Swipe, Delete	30-40
5	Poor Visibility	41-51
6	Strangers Everywhere	52-58
7	Golden	59-70
8	Thunder Only Happens When It's Raining	71-79
9	Street Ladder	80-89

ACKNOWLEDGMENTS

It was during my Masters I realised that the expression *'this is a chapter of my life'* wasn't good enough for me. My life comprises of several short stories, each filled with characters, moments, and themes too rich to be condensed. So, to all those who have played a role in any of the short stories of my life - family, romantically, academically, professionally - thank you. You are an integral part of my narrative.

PAPROĆ

The yellow, wilted fern cradles into my chest as my fists collide against the door. I hit the wood so hard I think it'll come off at its hinges. There's a delicate pitter-patter of feet on the other side of the door.

I lean into the peephole, 'Open up!'

The door finally opens and Olivia's face hides behind the dangling chain of her lock.

'For goodness sake Olivia, it's me!'

'I know it's you Orla. Do you *know* what time it is?'

It's 6 a.m. The rising sun bursts through the clouds along the skyline. The fern tickles my chin.

'Why did you let it die?'

'What?'

I stick the plant out, pushing it into the gap. 'You let it die. Why did you let it die?'

'Orla, you've been away for a while...' A tight wrinkle stretches across Olivia's silicone face.

'Look at it!' I push the plant between the gap, but it slips from my fingers. The pot shatters, mud spills and crisp leaves break. I'm on the floor, using my shaking fingers to rake the mud, the pot, the plant. I'm crying.

'Jesus Christ Orla! You let it die too!'

Broken pieces of ceramic skid into my lap as she kicks them out of her apartment. She tells me that she has a plane to catch later today, that if I'm going to have a mental breakdown about a plant, to take it elsewhere. I'm left in the hallway, the dead plant in my hands, fingers stained with mud.

I chuck the plant in the bins behind the flats, trying to remove the grime beneath my fingernails. I managed to compose myself before Olivia had the chance to call security, but my face is still puffy and lined with dry tears. Salt stains my upper lip. My phone notifies me that I have two voicemails. I dial and, of course, it's Mickie.

PAPROĆ

'Ms Longwater, your virtual calendar says you're back from the Lake District today but I'm still yet to hear anything about your meetings, so I'm just going to reschedule them for next week...I really hope you're okay Ms Longwater. Please, let me know. Oh, also you've received a bunch of flowers at the office with no note.'

The voice on the second message is softer. 'Orla please, please unblock—'

I press three and the voicemail is deleted. The streets are beginning to bustle with commuters on their way to work. There has to be a pub open somewhere.

Wherever one is, I can't find it. It's seven o'clock in the morning and every bar and pub opens their doors at eleven. A particularly dodgy one opens at ten. So I do something I haven't done since I was fourteen: I go to a corner shop, buy some cider and trek to the park. I walk down the path, ignoring dog walkers who try to smile at me, my plastic bag swinging at my knees. The first few benches I walk past are occupied, so I venture onto the grass, spotting a welcoming tree. I lean my body against the trunk and fall onto the damp grass that is coated in the early morning dew. The can exhales with a loud *tsk* as it opens. I realise how dry my mouth is as the cider touches my lips.

I finish the first without taking a breath. I open another.

I'm pretty drunk when I finish my fourth can. The tree trunk keeps me upright and steady. I didn't see any of my employees on their morning commute, I think they'd have too much to say if they saw their CEO drunk on a Tuesday in a park at – *Jesus* – 8:02 a.m. I open my fifth can.

I wake up to the cider spilling all over me. It slips through my fingers and the can empties its entire contents over me. I rush to stand, totally missing my footing and, head-over-arse, trip. This is also when I notice that my little bag of alcohol is missing. On all fours, I crawl around the trunk, thinking perhaps a branch has pinched my alcohol. Dizzy from going around in circles on my hands and knees, I realise some ballsy teenager or desperate alcoholic may have probably stolen it. I give up searching. Whoever it was has done me a favour. The pubs are open now anyway.

I reek of wet grass, mud and a brewery. It's safe to say, I need to wash. Too far away from my jet-stream jacuzzi bathtub, a toilet sink will have to do the trick.

'You need to purchase,' the woman behind the bar barks at me, staring at me through her overgrown fringe. She repeats herself as she sprays the counter with what smells like pine car freshener. Somehow her voice is even colder than before.

'I'm going to purchase.' She continues to stare at me. 'Right, well how about you pour me an old-fashioned on the rocks and I'll have it when I'm fresh and dandy.' The woman remains unmoved. 'Jesus-*fucking*-Christ.' I reach into my pocket pulling out my credit card, sliding it across the bar. 'Am I excused now?' I receive a slight nod and dash to the loos.

My curls now damp from the grimy sink water, I sit down on a stool. The old-fashioned is sat on top of a wooden coaster as the bartender inspects my card. Her eyes do not move from the American Express. If she studies the numbers hard enough maybe she'll go home and buy herself some nicer clothes.

'Nice bar,' I say not even turning to look at the dull and depressing décor.

'Orla Longwater, I recognise that name. Aren't you some kind of big shot who buys companies?'

'Depends,' I grab my drink. 'Are you an owner of one of the businesses I neglected to save?'

The bartender shakes her head, 'Nope, just married to a man who works in one of your warehouses.' The wedding ring on her finger doesn't even attempt to sparkle. 'That will make you my husband's boss's boss's… boss?' Her voice trails off. She hands me my card, 'I better not piss you off.'

'Too late,' I say lightly, smiling into my glass.

'Shouldn't you be sat up in a penthouse somewhere?'

Yep, absolutely. I take a hearty swig of my drink, finishing it.

'Depends. Is this beauty for sale?' This time I actually look around. It's as though the designer didn't know enough about one era, so has tried to amalgamate four decades into one cramped room.

'Trust me, if I got the money for this place I'd sell it to you right now. But I'm afraid I'm not the owner, only the bartender.'

'Well, it's a good thing I'm here for a drink and not another business.' I push my empty glass towards her.

The conversation between me and the woman ceases as she goes to the cellar to grab another bottle of whiskey. Faced with a purple-lit mirror, amongst the bottles of liquor, my face distorts.

'You look like you're in pain,' she states upon returning. Is it that obvious?

I lift my drink after she pours it. 'To my first vacation in two thousand nine hundred and twenty days.' The whiskey wets my lips.

'Wow,' she breathes. 'I guess congratulations is in order, any special occasion?'

They say it's always easy to talk to a stranger, that's why I almost say it. Her deep hazel eyes look at me expectantly and I notice – despite the stern voice – how gentle her face is.

'Excuse me,' I say finding my voice as I stumble off the stool. I'm sure she's seen it a hundred times. Someone darting to the toilets, trying to look like they're not about to be sick.

In the ladies, I retch violently. It isn't until I stop puking I feel the cramps. It isn't until I look down, I see the blood piling in the crotch of my jeans.

They told me I'd most likely stop bleeding between seven to fourteen days. I even stayed in Lake District for three weeks to make sure. Yet, here I am, sitting on the toilet, crimson liquid spilling and staining the bowl. My underwear, sanitary towel and trousers ruined. The cramps nearly make me double over. I start crying and then I get angry - crying makes me angry. It makes me hot, flustered, and red in the face. It feels like all I've done recently is switch between burning rage and burning sadness. Before, crying was few and far between. Often, I forced myself to watch films like *Marley and Me* just to remind myself that something, anything, was inside of me. My arms wrap around my stomach, tightening. The hinges on the door beyond the cubical squeak. I swallow my tears. If there is anything worse than crying, it's crying in front of someone.

'Uh, Ms Long…Orla… Are you okay? If you're vomiting, I beg you just aim for the bowl.'

Silence. I'm biting on my lower lip, trying to ride the wave of a cramp. My vision starts spotting.

'Right then,' she sighs. 'I'll check on you—'

'Wait!' The sound of my voice carries through the cubical. 'I-I…' *Fuck*. 'I need help.' I lean forward, pull the lock and let the door swing. Her eyes flash wide.

'Are you…' She stares at my bloodied thigh and crotch.

'I had an-'

At the same time I say *abortion*, she says *miscarriage*. I don't know whose voice is heavier.

'Oh, okay.'

I should have kept my mouth shut. She storms out without another word. As I am faced with the back of her head, for a moment all I can picture is Archie. Archie walking away from me, making me do all this by myself. The tears return but so does the woman, holding a thick black towel.

'Let's get you cleaned up, shall we?'

She leads me upstairs to the flat above the pub. Her name is Edie. She explains the owner won't be back until later, that she has a key for emergencies. I'm thankful that the bleeding has now slowed, almost entirely stopped. My thighs stick together from the tangy blood, but I continue to waddle as if any minute the floodgates will reopen. She directs me into the bathroom and I assume she'll leave me be, but instead she pushes the blue shower curtain back and switches the water on.

'Go on,' she motions to the shower and I hesitate. She rolls her eyes turning around. 'I won't look but I'm not leaving,' she crosses her arms. 'Last thing you need is to pass out and hit your head on the tap.'

I strip naked and when I get in the water is hot. The liquid stains red as it runs down my body. My legs start shaking and when I'm only moments from collapsing, a gentle hand is placed into mine. Edie guides me to the shower floor. I'm crying. She too has tears in her eyes. It reminds me of Archie when I told him the condom hadn't worked. He sobbed loudly. When I told him I booked the appointment, his eyes became dry. He even uttered the phrase, 'Great choice'.

'I know it was my choice.'

'Doesn't mean it was easy,' Edie whispers, tucking a strand of hair behind my ear. 'Doesn't mean it didn't hurt to choose.'

I haven't started bleeding again, but I continue to sit on the shower floor while Edie perches on the toilet lid. The bathroom is full of steam and her hair is damp.

'You don't need the hospital,' she says, reaching for the soap.

'Are you also a nurse?'

A soft smile doesn't reach her eyes, 'No.'

I soap hard between my legs. Archie always loved kissing me there, told me it's where my skin was softest.

'Where is he?' Edie's eyebrow is raised. 'The baby daddy.'

I try not to grimace at the suggestion there is even a baby to daddy.

'Dubai probably.'

Archie hadn't forced me to make the appointment, but he also made it very clear that the other option, where we pick out colour schemes and order a pram, was simply not an option.

'It was my decision.' The soap lathers me in bubbles. 'I know you're thinking I'm an evil monster.'

'Not at all,' she looks at the white tiled wall. 'I think you had to make a difficult choice, but a choice that is right for you and your life.'

My life: the penthouses, the spontaneous business trips, the long meetings, working in different countries. A baby, no matter how hard I tried to squeeze it, never fit into any of those spaces.

'You're kind.'

She finally meets my eye, 'And you're pruney,' she points to my fingers.

For the first time in weeks, I laugh. It sounds foreign. I am however silenced by a slamming door. Edie, standing quickly, curses under her breath, informing me that the boss is back and to stay put. It's only when she leaves that I realise how loud the water is.

Edie's arguing with the boss. They're shouting in Polish and I'm hovering by the door, ear pressed against the wood in only a towel.

'Okay, we're going!' Edie yells, now in English. I step back only in the nick of time before the door pushes open. Edie, slightly red in the face, walks in with a pile of clothes in her hands. She body scans me.

'Are you okay?'

'Are you?'

She dismisses the question with a wave of a hand.

'These are for you.' With the tips of my fingers, I pinch the hot pink tank top and bring it to my chest. 'His girlfriend is… young.' Edie pulls a face as though there is a bad taste in her mouth. 'We've got to go.'

'We?' She nods. I shake my head. 'No, you stay.'

'Boss's instruction. I mean, you can ask him yourself. That is, if you can speak Polish.'

'Mogę spróbować.' I butcher the pronunciation but smile nonetheless.

PAPROĆ

'Businesswoman, eh?' Edie smirks. 'Now get changed.'

Edie shuffles me out through the back door, purposefully avoiding the bar and boss. I'm expecting it to be dark when I step out, but I'm greeted by the light, grey sky. I peel my phone out of the plastic bag that holds my bloodied clothes, the clock reading 16:18.

Edie points to the bus stop across the road, informing me it'll take us to the underground in three stops. I haven't gotten the bus since I was in school and I don't plan on changing that anytime soon. I wiggle my phone at her.

She's inching left and right on the leather seats of the taxi. Even when she exhales loudly, she's stiff.

'It's nice,' she mutters. 'Seeing life on the other side of the river.'

It's a weird expression. All the same, my spine straightens.

'I've worked hard to be where I am.'

'I never said you didn't,' she looks out the tinted window. 'It doesn't matter anyway, we all bleed the same.' My crossed legs tighten. I wonder where Archie is.

'Are you planning on tucking me in bed?' I laugh as we enter the lift.

'Depends,' Edie zips her jacket up. 'If you have a king-sized then no, too many corners too far away from each other.'

The lift doors begin to shut, but not before the sound of pitter-pattering heels and skidding of a suitcase whizz past the elevator. Luckily, even in the cheetah hot pants, Olivia does not clock me.

'A friend?'

'I woke her up at six in the morning crying about a dead plant.'

A deep snort bursts from Edie's nose. 'Hormones will do that to you.'

As the lift climbs the flats, we laugh.

PAPROĆ

We step out of the lift and a man is sitting cross-legged leaning on a door. His head is hanging in his lap and he's breathing heavily.

'Archie?' Orla breathes. The name carries down the hall. He stirs and wobbles onto his feet, still half-asleep. He is handsome as Orla is beautiful, in the stereotypical kind of way.

'Orla.' He has a French accent.

There's a long pause I decide to break by lifting my hand.

'Edie.' The sound of my voice makes Orla almost flinch. That's when I decide it's best to leave. 'I'll let you both be.'

Orla does not suggest otherwise, instead she nods, her hands reaching towards Archie.

'Wait!' Orla's voice calls just as the lift doors reopen. She rushes into me, wrapping her arms around me. She smells like soap. 'Thank you Edie, thank you for everything.' We pull away from each other just in time for me to enter the lift before the doors close. The last thing I see is Orla and her dark round eyes, a small sad smile stretching across her face.

By the time I get on the bus, ready for an hour's journey, it's dark. My phone is dead so I am unable to call Jakub and tell him I'm going to be home late.

At the third stop a woman with an industrial pram clambers on. I look away as the woman and baby sit in front of me, averting my attention to the bustling city. Then, the baby starts crying. It's a new-born, three months at the very most and her cries vibrate through my body. Some passengers grunt and nestle their earphones in tighter, others coo at the sad baby. I ache. There's an emptiness inside of me I try to ignore, and even when I manage to block out the baby's tears, all I can think of is Orla and the blood. No matter how many times you wash, it never fades.

I walk through the door and am greeted by Jakub's open arms.

'Petal,' his voice is loud. 'Where have you been?' The house reeks of stew. The pungent scent of meat carries into the air. He offers me an unopened cider. It's room temperature as I bring it to my lips.

'I nearly called work,' Jakub stalks off to the kitchen. *Nearly*, meaning he didn't. 'What kept you?'

'The pub was busier than I expected it to be.' I fall onto the sofa, the cushions absorbing my weight. I'm about to kick off my shoes when I spot blood on the soles. Before Jakub comes back into the room, I'm dashing to the bedroom, dropping my clothes into the wash basket, shoes included. I reach into the cupboard for some new pyjamas, noticing a cardboard box on the shelf that had not been there this morning. I pull at it and a wooden rattle tumbles to the floor, narrowly missing my toes. I know what he's done. I know why he didn't call work; he was busy cleaning.

I grab the rattle, which is cold in my fingers and, when I open the nursery door that has been closed for far too long, a pit falls into my stomach. The crib is dismantled, the toys gone. The only thing that remains is the rocking chair and flower mobile that is slowly twirling in the air.

'Jakub.' My voice is a whisper, as if all the air has been punched out of me. I take a deep breath. 'JAKUB!' He enters the room as I'm pacing through it. He says nothing but lowers his eyes. 'What have you—' I'm stammering. 'Why have you—'

'You know why.'

I point to the crib, 'Build it.'

'Edie.'

'Build it! NOW!' I kneel, intent on building the thing myself. Jakub wraps his arms around me trying to peel me off the ground. 'Get off me!' He steps away as the tears fall into my lap. 'You had no right!'

'Edie, you know we can't try again. It's...' His voice fades. 'We can't risk it.' His arms wrap around me again and I do not fight it. Instead, I fall into them.

'We can,' I whisper, lowering the pieces of wood. 'We can.'

He returns my kiss, my tongue meeting his and my palm cupping his face. He pulls my body closer. I guide his hand between my legs and his fingers traces the edges of my underwear.

'No, Edie.' He shakes his head, pulling away. The glimmer of light reflecting in his pupils tells me that he will not change his mind.

'Please,' I cry. 'Please.'

He gets up off the floor, dusting himself off. 'I'm going to check dinner, we need to eat.'

I want to storm out, but it's dark and our neighbourhood isn't safe. So instead, we sit opposite each other at the dining table in absolute silence. Jakub's shift starts at midnight, so I know I only have to bear this for another four hours. I have not touched my dinner. Jakub, on the other hand, is scooping the stew into his mouth. Even though it's liquid, he's chewing loudly. The stew dribbles down his chin.

'What?' His mouth is full. 'What are you staring at?'

I'm hurting. My womb is empty. Help me.

'You repulse me.'

His eyes roll, 'Very mature Edie.' He continues scooping.

'Just stop!' My fists pound on the table. My untouched stew spills on the white cloth. Jakub, reaching for a napkin, knocks his cider over. He stands, his brow narrowed, jaw tight. I cross my arms and the vein in Jakub's neck pulsates.

'I lost them too Edie, but I nearly lost you as well.' He wipes his mouth. 'And as much as I want a baby, I *need* you.' Tears nearly spill from his eyes but he glances away before they fall. 'I'm going to work early. I think we need some space.' He pushes his chair away from under him, 'And *you* can clean this up.'

I'm rocking back and forth staring at the desolate room, the rattle in my hand, the blanket up to my chin. Slow, delicate tears roll down my face. The last time I sat in the rocking chair, I was five months pregnant with Twinkle. We were so close. The house phone in the hallway rings, but I let it go to voicemail, I know it's Jakub. I expect him to hang up, but after the automated message, his voice bursts alive.

'Petal! I tried phoning you but your phone, it is still dead.' There's a loud murmuring and, in broken English, Jakub instructs people in the background to shut up. 'The warehouse has been given a bonus from the CEO Edie! A HUGE bonus! I can't believe it. It's just what we need petal, a break. Just a little break. We've been given the night off so the boys are going to celebrate. I'll be home earlier than usual. Aren't we lucky?'

Through the closed window overlooking the city, there's a full moon. A cramp tightens in my lower stomach.

'So lucky,' I say to the dismantled crib. I close my eyes and rock myself to sleep.

SEASONAL SKIES

I hold the bed sheets. If I look close enough, I can see the stains. My fingers wrap around the fabric tighter. The washing machine is open, but my eyes keep darting to the drawer. I try to breathe, but the oxygen is too thick, it tightens my throat.

'Come on, Charlie.'

Beyond the windows overlooking the city, the sky is darkening. The sun is probably setting, but it is impossible to tell from the thick, grey clouds that have been spewing droplets of rain all day. I twist the sheet in my hand and that's when I see it, a lipstick mark. I'm running to the drawer, trying not to slip on the cotton tangling between my feet. The scissors feel lighter than the sheet, which I waste no time cutting through. When the scissors are no longer enough to settle the rage that is burning, I use my hands. The ripping of the sheet echoes through the empty apartment. I stop ripping, drop the bed sheet and start crying instead.

I want to clean the apartment and simultaneously destroy it at the same time. So, instead, I sit on the sofa staring at the muted TV. The night has quietly and silently crept upon me. I am saturated in mostly darkness. The living room is hazy from the lavender and white sage incense smoke. It's meant to cleanse bad energy. It makes my lungs ache.

Footsteps in the hallway make my spine stiffen and I feel as though I have been sitting on concrete. Although many footsteps have trailed up and down the apartment hallway all day, I immediately recognise his. They're heavy.

'Charlie-girl,' he coos like he has every day for the past twelve years.

I'm crying, my face sitting in the palms of my hands. His footsteps hesitate on the wooden floor by the living room door. For a split second, I think he'll leave. I'm surprised to find myself hoping he does. As soon as I see those rounded blue eyes, it's going to be real, more real than the stains and the lipstick mark. The door swings open,

'Why are you sitting in the dark?'

He switches the light on. It's blinds me. I shield my eyes from the orange light. He always knows when I'm upset, a 'useless poker face' he once called it. I guess that was his way of saying that one of us is a better liar than the other. He extends his grubby hands out. Grease and car oil line his oval fingernails. How had his fingers touched her in our bed?

'No.' I bring my knees to my chest, shaking my head. 'Don't... You-you broke a rule.'

'What?' He attempts to approach again.

'I said you broke a rule!' My voice hardens. 'You brought her into our goddamn home.' I pinch the bridge of my nose, expecting him to immediately grovel and say that he is sorry. I am met with only silence. I crane my neck to look up at him through the gaps of my fingers.

'Charlie,' he sighs. 'I broke more than just that rule.' His pale face is red and blotchy as if he has had too many drinks. I know it is not alcohol he is drunk on. 'Why don't I make us a hot drink?' Before I can answer, he turns his back on me and wanders off into the kitchen.

His hands are steady as he pours a teaspoon of sugar into the mug. The rage burns from the pit of my stomach and spreads across my skin like wildfire.

'Are you not even—'

'Oat or soya milk?' He interrupts me. It momentarily extinguishes the heat in my throat.

'Oat.'

He fetches the milk from the fridge, briefly looking at me, but as fast as he does, he looks away. Is it shame or guilt? My poker face may suck, but his is impeccable. By the third clang of the teaspoon against the ceramic mug, I slam my hands on the counter.

'Enough!' I cry out. 'You don't get to waltz in here and say nothing, not even a—'

I am silenced as he opens the bin to throw away the teabag. He's staring at the bed sheet that has been shredded and stuffed amongst rotting food. He pulls it out and examines it. His index finger rubs over the lipstick stain. I imagine that's how he played with her real lips. He doesn't look at me when he says, 'I love her Charlie. I'm in love with her.'

I consider - for only a moment- how long it would take, or how much strength I would need, to wrap the sheet around his neck. He dumps it back into the bin, reaching for my mug on the counter.

'Wash your hands.' I demand. He looks at me as if it is *me* who has just ruined our marriage. 'I said…' My words slow. 'Wash your lipstick-cum-stained hands, before you give me my damn tea.'

He washes his hands as I clamber onto the metal stool. The cold makes me shiver. I'm still hoping to see his fingers shake, but they're steady as he places the cup of tea in front of me. There's a clap of thunder behind me as I ask, 'What's her name?'

'Don't,' he says softly. 'Don't do this to yourself.'

I laugh - it's empty and hollow and it hurts my chest. 'No-no,' I wiggle my finger. '*You* did this to me. Let's not mix this up.'

'You're right.'

'I know I am.'

His rounded eyes flare wide as if to say, *really, the last word?* I do not apologise. We sip on our teas despite them being far too hot, but I think I know what burning pain we both prefer.

'So, I'm going to assume you broke our 'no-more-than-twice' rule too?' He doesn't need to answer, so I prod further. 'How long?'

'Six months.'

I inhale sharply, 'Did you meet her friends?'

He nods.

'Did she meet ours?'

He shakes his head hard and fast as if I had just asked something preposterous.

'Oh?' I'm genuinely surprised. 'So you'll bring her into

our home but won't let her hear one of Dave's jokes?' There's another crack of thunder, right above the flat.

'I didn't want them telling...' His voice fades away as he speaks into the mug.

'Telling me?' The venom on my tongue stings. I want to spit it all in his direction, but I am lost for words. It is as though the venom burns through them before they leave my mouth and only I am poisoned.

He follows behind me as I walk through the living room.

'Come on Charlie, the idea of an open relationship was doomed from the start. Don't kid yourself it was going to end in any other way. You should have never listened to that quack-'

'Do not call Stevie that!' I stop in the middle of the room, so we are face-to-face. 'Why then?'

'Why what?'

'Why the *fuck* did you agree to it then? If you knew it would be a disaster.'

'Because I wanted you to be happy!' He's beginning to raise his voice. 'You made the suggestion and it seemed like it would make you happy so I went along with it, but I knew it was a matter of time until you found someone else.'

I hold my finger up to him, 'That was never the goal.'

'Then what was the goal?'

I recite Stevie's words, 'to experience more with the person I love!'

'Love?' He gasps. 'Where? *Where* is this love? I can't see it, I can't touch it.' His voice breaks. 'I most certainly can't feel it.'

And there they are, tears in his eyes. He has not wept for falling in love with another woman, but he weeps for the love that he lost. With another clap of thunder, the lights momentarily flicker before turning off. We are left in the dark, with only our tears as company.

I feel his presence lingering behind me like an intravenous I want to rip from my veins. I grab things as I go, photo frames, books, anything I can get my hands on, and throw them to the floor. He shouts my name, telling me not to be ridiculous. I don't stop moving until I'm in our darkened bedroom. Usually the light from the city bursts into the room, but even the outside world is dark. The only light comes from the moon, which is desperately trying to peek through the thick clouds. It's doing an awful job, I only see shadows. But I know the way around the room enough, and my eyes have become somewhat accustomed to the eternal night. I drop my knees onto the carpet, hauling the suitcase from underneath the bed, dragging a wave of dust out along with it. It makes me sneeze. I'm offered no blessing, despite him hovering behind me.

I yank the suitcase and a shoebox tumbles out, a pile of photos spread across the carpet. He offers to use his phone as a source of light, but I pay no attention as I reach for a photo. As the white light bursts from his hands, the photo shines. It's from our first date. One where he's looking at me, smiling. He probably looks at her the same way now.

'It's here,' I whisper, wiggling the photo. 'The love.' My hand points to the wardrobe that we had built together many years ago, 'It's there and it's in the streets too, and the bookcase, and the photo frames and in every minute that has ticked by for the past twelve years.'

He lowers himself onto the carpet, dropping the phone so the light is shining from beneath us. 'Then why? Why this idea to sleep with other people?'

I try to respond but I cry instead. My fingers curl, crumpling the photo in my palms. I want to tell him that we had fallen in love too young. We had missed so many experiences that we both, or so I thought, wanted to have. Our relationship had become stagnant, and we no longer ignited passion from our fingertips. But instead, through my guttural sobs, I say,

'I thought you would choose me when the sun had set. I thought you would always choose me.'

He opens his arms and I find myself falling into them. My face is in his shoulder and I'm crying into his clothes. The rain and wind outside intensify. For a moment, I think the window might shatter.

I don't know how long we sit on our bedroom floor. I think we fall asleep leaning on the bedframe as we are startled by the light that illuminates our apartment and the city outside. The power is back on. I pull myself out of his arms, the tears on my cheeks are now dry.

'You've got to go.' He doesn't reply as he stumbles onto his feet, tucking his phone into his pocket. 'You can stay at hers.' He doesn't argue, but he hovers under the arch and rubs his palm up and down the floral-patterned wallpaper. Air blowing from his nose,

'I can feel it now,' he takes one glance at me. 'The love.'

I smile but it doesn't reach my eyes. 'Too little too late.' I lift the photo that has been and still is in my hands. I rip it in half.

PEN & PAPER

Beige, the floor, the chairs, the walls, the ceiling, even the goddamn people. Not literally of course. Some have bright blue eyes or other dazzling features. There's even one woman who looks like a drumstick lolly with blue and green hair. She looks like she belongs here.

'You know, I think all of us here are really brave,' the woman who introduced herself as Anita says. I'm surprised the smug bitch isn't wearing a white coat and holding a clipboard. Instead, she wears a buttoned green cardigan and a plait falls delicately over her shoulder like a scarf made of gold, but that's not the best part. The best part is, on top of the green cardigan and beside her luscious hair, between her perky breasts, sits a dainty silver crucifix. By being here she's doing her one holy deed of the day. I bet she graduated from somewhere like Oxford. Mummy and Daddy probably paid for her accommodation and bought her a brand new Fiat 500 when she did mediocre on her exams.

'We're brave because maybe, *just maybe*, being here is tricky for some of us.' She probably shops at Waitrose. 'And we're all going to be brave, *together*.' Nope, Marks and Spencer's.

The Drumstick Lady snorts, 'This is group therapy, not Girl Scouts.'

There's a low vibrational chuckle from everyone in the circle. Anita flushes red, pats down her skirt and recrosses her legs.

'Of course,' she stammers, 'but we must identify our bravery to prepare us to share. I'll go first—'

I look away from Little Miss Anita. Who is she trying to kid with those Louboutin heels and diamond rings? My eyes lock with an older man in the circle. He's wearing an ill-fitted grey suit. It looks like, once upon a time, it might've fit him. He proceeds to lift his hand to his head, his fingers imitating a gun, pulling the trigger. His head droops and his dark eyes cross. I lower my gaze into my lap, trying to stifle a chuckle. However, Little Miss Anita's voice, Little Miss Anita's story, begins to occupy all the spaces of the city hall and all the tiny crevices of my mind. My skin begins to tingle. My leg begins to bounce.

I consider poking, no – jamming, my index fingers in my ears. I've sat through worse than this, much worse. Eight hours of tattooing for example, where the needles punctured my back until it felt like a dragon was breathing on my skin. I had wanted to leave then but I hadn't, and it had paid off. Maybe this would be one of those times. So I'll sit here like I had in the parlour and take it, take the pain.

'Did you try to leave him?' The police officer repeats. 'Did you at least try?'

I'm on my feet, pushing the chair with my calves until it crashes to the floor. Anita's doe eyes batter in my direction. I guess I'm not brave, huh?

Under my breath, I mutter some lame excuse like I've left the oven on at home or I've forgotten to feed the cat, and I grab my handbag from the floor, almost tripping on it as I do. Anita's nasal voice vibrates in the background telling me I should try and stay. She tells me that staying will be good for me, but in her voice I can only hear the police officer's and he was right. I should've left.

With my shaking fingers, it takes three attempts to light my cigarette. The cold air feels nice against my clammy skin as I stand in the city hall car park. Even though a gentle breeze pulsates through the air, my hair is plastered to the back of my neck. The smoke in my lungs feels lighter than the oxygen around me. With only a lamppost as my source of light, I try to allocate the cars to the fucked-up owners in the city hall. I don't spot a Fiat 500.

The door I exited only moments ago swings open and shut. In my peripheral vision, I spot the baggy suit. A super-king cigarette hangs out of his mouth, and he takes my zippo lighter with no thanks. The aroma of menthol wafts into my face.

'Pussied out then?'

'Watch it.' I hiss, my voice empty and hollow. With the cigarette in his mouth, he lifts his hands as if he were surrendering himself to the enemy on the front line. I start walking off.

'Oi sunshine!' I don't stop, that is until he says, 'I'm outside too!'

I pause under the lamppost. I glance back, the orange light makes the lines around his eyes soft. He looks younger than he had in the harsh, white light of the city hall.

'Do you fancy a drink?' I call out.

He smiles.

I escort him into the pub. Through the thick cloud of smoke, his eyes illuminate. Bottles of liquor parade the shelves, all the while people are dealing pills or snorting lines. By the time we sit down, he is glowing.

'How the hell—'

'Never heard of a back door pub?'

'Of course I have.' He's unable to hide his grin. 'I'm just wondering how the hell I haven't discovered this gem myself.'

Rick approaches the table, tucking his little notepad in his jeans, he recites my usual order. 'And for...' As he points to my companion I realise I do not even know his name.

'Lawrence.' The suit makes sense now. 'I'll take a pint of Moretti.' He shoots a quick wink at me, 'And two tequila shots for good measure.'

As Rick walks away, Lawrence sticks his tongue out. Even through the smoke and low light, yellow stains are visible on his teeth.

'I know what you're thinking, it's pretentious.' His face creases as though he has a bad taste in his mouth. '*Lawrence* the lost lawyer.'

'Lawyer?'

'Emphasis on the 'lost', doll face. The sniffer dogs got me good. Found a gram of packet in my pocket.' He pulls out his cigarettes from his jacket. 'What about you? Name? Story?'

'*Betty*, Betty who got beat.'

Lawrence's mouth tightens together and he rests both of his hands on his heart.

'Jesus, that must've been hard.' I'm about to tell him to quit the act when he adds, 'Your parents must have really hated you to call you Betty.' A husky laughter rolls from his chest.

'Well, it's a good thing my name's Nellie then,' I lean back in my chair. 'Arsehole.'

'Hey, it's just some good ol' healthy projection.' He lifts his hands as if he's surrendering again. 'I wish my parents hated me, I am where I am because they loved me a little bit *too* much.'

Damn.

'Father or mother?'

'Father.'

Double damn.

Cigarette in hand, he points at me. 'Let me guess, uncle?'

It's as if we're talking about the weather or the price of a pint of milk.

'No, no incest I'm afraid.'

Our drinks arrive. We make a toast to Little Miss Anita and her boyfriend: the Lord and Saviour Jesus Christ.

'I can't imagine we're missing much,' Lawrence pulls out another cigarette whilst having the last puff of his first one. 'She's probably suggesting to journal feelings or try downloading a meditation app.'

I take a hearty swig of my beer, 'Or maybe telling everyone to try exercising.'

'Jesus, where do you think she got her license from? Wikipedia?'

'Or her priest.'

'Can't be any worse than the first therapist I had,'

Lawrence reveals. 'The bitch told me to write a letter to the person who *hurt me*. Unsure how she expected an eleven-year-old to send a letter to their fuckin-daddy without explaining that to dear Mumsy.' He pauses. 'Not that dear Mumsy didn't know what was happening anyway.' Lawrence smashes his smoked cigarette into the ashtray with more force than he had the others. I flinch.

'Shit,' he freezes. 'Sorry.'

'Why the fuck are you flinching!' He screams 'Do I scare you or something? I'll show you something to be fucking scared of!'

'Don't apologise,' I laugh. Lawrence hesitates.
Laugh. Please laugh.
His gaze softens, 'Do you think anyone else wanted to slash Anita's tires or do you think it was just us?'

'Anyone with their head screwed on right will have slashed all four by now.'

Lawrence shakes his head. 'Three, doll face. Four is covered by insurance.'

We make another toast.

Lawrence and I exchange numbers as we stumble down the alleyway. He offers to walk me home and I decline. The streets are mostly empty and the illegal taser attached to my key chain makes the occasional street wanderer just a wanderer. I've barely been away from Lawrence for five minutes when my phone in my back pocket vibrates.

```
R u home? Could've kept u warm 2nite
```

I laugh and reply,

```
    Would rather write that letter tbh
```

I tuck my phone away as I enter my apartment complex. I can't remember the last time I wrote a letter. Oh wait, that's not true, I was eight years old and the recipient had been Santa Claus. I tried posting it without a stamp to the North

Pole, and the person behind the kiosk laughed at me, informing me that I should have a word with my mother. That's how I found out Santa Claus wasn't real.

As I enter the lift a fast-approaching male makes me jump, gesturing for me to hold it for him. He thanks me. I nestle myself against the opposing wall.

'Floor?' he asks.

'Ninth.'

I finger the taser on my key ring, cold against my burning fingertips.

'Been as busy day for you as it has been for me?' he questions.

I don't recognise him. I've never seen him in my apartment complex before.

'I guess.' I look at my phone.

Ding.

We hit the ninth floor. I dash out as he says goodbye. When the lift doors close, I rush down the stairs to level six.

With the front door double padlocked, I step over clothes that are scattered on the floor like rose petals. I trail into the bathroom, again locking myself in. Used floss hangs over the sink edge and toothpaste stains the plug. I stare into my reflection until my eyes are heavy.

'I love you, Nellie.' He pulls me into him, caressing my hot aching cheek.

'I love you,' I cry into his wine-stained lips. I love him so much, it hurts.

Immersed under the cold tap, I can't tell the difference between my tears and the water.

'This is stupid,' I say to the pen as if it could reply. 'Ludicrous.'

I flatten the creases out of the paper. The smoke from the ashtray swirls into the air. The pen rests on the paper.

Dear

I have to write his name, of course I do, it's a letter. I take a long and heavy drag. I should throw the piece of paper away, go and have a shower instead, wash the remnants of the shitty day away. But no matter how hot I set the temperature, it'll never be hot enough to burn him away, so maybe burning him isn't the answer. I grab my phone.

'Doll face?' he answers after the second dial. 'Are you okay?'

I shake my head, tears falling onto the blank paper. He asks again.

'I'm-I'm holding a pen.'

'Ah, I see.'

'And I can't…I can't even write his goddamn name.'

There's a moment of silence followed by a gentle sizzle that creeps into my ear, a cigarette I assume.

'I'll stay on the phone as you write it.'

'I don't know.'

'Be brave,' Lawrence whispers back.

My pen hits the paper.

✉

Grey, the floor, the curtains, the walls, the ceiling, even the world outside. So much for a heatwave in summer. I'm not particularly bothered by it, it doesn't make a difference, the day will be the same. That is until Mam's voice hollers from the hallway.

'Get up! You're going to school today!'

I groan and duck my head under the duvet until my face is warm from the condensation of my breath. I thought I'd have at least another week. Mam hurdles through my door, nearly tripping on a mountain of dirty clothes.

'Jesus Mimi!'

'Don't use the Lord's name in vain.' I poke my head out.

'I'm sorry,' she breathes, kicking dirty underwear away from her ankles. 'I told the Headmaster you were going back today.'

'Tell him you made a mistake,' I turn my back on her. My room is a mess, but my bedside table is immaculate. The crucifix stands tall beside a single, half-melted candle and a photo of me sitting on Daddy's lap at Christmas. Two concert tickets are pinned onto the frame. I had been far too young to have seen the death metal band, but Daddy was always super charming and persuasive, coaxing security into letting me in.

'Mimi, you're going to school today.' Mam's voice is hard. I know she won't budge.

I obviously don't go to school. Mam should've known that, unless she walked me directly to each lesson, maybe dragged me into maths, I was never going to go. I'm halfway through Metallica's *The Black* album when I find myself on His doorstep. It's no surprise. Daddy always said we gravitate back home and home is where Daddy is. I approach his grave, only metres away from the entrance of the Church, imagining that's how Daddy will greet me in Heaven, right by the entrance. The flowers on his grave are still vibrant and the earth is freshly disturbed. I settle onto the ground when there's a heckling from beyond the gates. I needn't even look to know who the voices belong to, Chloe and her posse.

I haven't heard from anyone at school since Daddy's death, not even an *'I'm sorry'* from the all-silent group chat. It's not that they don't know about it. The news had been posted on Facebook, notifying everyone in the local area they had lost a valuable member of the church and community. I'm hoping by sitting in front of Daddy's cross they'll leave me well alone, but the gate creaks and murmurs vibrate. I'm unable to avoid it so, still sitting, I look over my shoulder and wave.

Chloe, chewing on blue bubble gum approaches, towering

over me. She pulls out a packet of cigarettes, places one between her lips and then motions for a member of the group to light it for her. Amongst the crowd, Markus steps forward. As he does, purposefully refusing to meet my eye, I am faced with the memory of Markus begging me for a handjob at the skatepark. Chloe takes a long drag on her lit cigarette, before pulling the gum out from her mouth and dropping it inches away from my legs, right on Daddy's grave. Pieces of the earth roll around the sickly blue bubble gum.

'You thought I wouldn't find out, didn't you? Asking *my* boyfriend for a handjob?' Will the piece of bubble gum sink to his coffin like the earth? 'You think I'm going to be nice to you because you lost your little daddy?' At his name, my eyes meet hers. Like a disease, a dark smirk spreads across her face. 'Everyone knows what he was *really* like anyway, the whole town does.'

'Chloe,' Markus caresses her shoulder.

'What?' Chloe bites. 'Why are you defending her?'

The argument ensues between the lovers, and Chloe makes a decision. On her last final drag, she drops the cigarette. The lit flame falls inches from my legs and the embers spit across Daddy's grave immersing him in heat, in flames, in Hell. Pouncing from the ground, I tackle Chloe. She's bigger than me, but I'm on top of her. Throwing my fists at her as if I were avenging and wrathful. I'm also screaming. As her knuckles aim for my face, I reach for the lit cigarette.

I wake up in the cemetery alone, my whole body aching. The group had pulled me off Chloe when the cigarette seared through her cheek and, although Chloe herself was too immobile to fight back, the rest of the group had no problem kicking and side-stomping me, knocking me unconscious.

Groaning with every step, I stumble back home. It takes me almost twice as long as it normally does as I try to blink through my swollen eye. I am greeted by the Postie on my doorstep who is reaching into his overflowed sack.

'Do you live here—' As his eyes meet mine he silences and looks me up and down. I am equal parts wet and covered in mud. 'You look like shit. Do you need me to call an ambulance or summin'?'

I shake my head.

He shrugs, 'Whatever you say.' He then hands me a wad of post. 'Hope your day gets better.'

I limp in, knowing full well I need to attend to my face before Mam gets home for her lunch break. I toss the post across the living room table, noticing a particular thick envelope with my address squiggled on the front. It's addressed to Daddy. I stare at it a moment, before picking it back up. My fingers tracing the stamp. I open it gently but it feels wrong, like I'm invading his personal space. It's a handwritten letter. In the corner there is a large red stain and as I edge my thumb against it, I realise it's red wine. There are blotches of ink where it looks like the writer has spilt their tears as they wrote it. Maybe this is their way of wishing my father a final farewell.

I glance to the end.

Sincerely, fuck you.
Nellie.

Fuck you? I shiver. Who's Nellie and why is she cursing my father? I start from the beginning.

The neighbours are nosey. They've been yelling over the fence for the past twenty minutes informing me they have rung my mother. They're worried I'm going to hurt myself. They're worried that I'm going to burn myself from the fire I have created. Maybe that's what I need, to purge myself from all the sin in my DNA. Smoke burns the hairs in my nostrils as I pour more lighter fluid. The concert tickets have incinerated and it's now tackling the Christmas photograph. When I see only ash, I pull the letter from my back pocket.

It's heavy and, amongst the crackle of flames, I begin to cry. I pry the envelope open, refusing to let my eye meet any more of its ugly truth and I pull the crucifix from my neck. The dead man on the cross glistens. I put it in the envelope before tossing it into the burning pit.

'Mimi!' my Mam's voice shrieks, pulling the patio door open. 'What the hell are you doing?!' She studies my face. 'My god, what happened to you?' She embraces me, prying the lighter fluid from my fingers, and me away from the heat.

I lick the dried blood from my lips, 'I'm sorry.'

She's flattening my hair, telling me it's okay but it isn't her I'm apologising to. It's to Nellie, for all the black eyes, broken wrists and ribs. For all the verbal abuse, mental torment, the Rape. The fire from behind grows.

DOWNLOAD, SWIPE, DELETE

Left

The last time I looked at the clock, it was 22:30. It's now 02:01 and my alarm is set to go off in four hours. I drop the phone on the duvet, massaging the cramp that's tightening through my palm. Ache radiates down my legs from lying like a foetus in bed for so long. The film I had been watching has stopped, the TV screen dark. I don't remember finishing the film. A pang resolves through my stomach, I have been sitting in darkness and silence for the whole night. A notification pings on my phone. It's probably Joel or Michael, Michael with the Two Cats, not Michael the Freelancer. Although I want to see who it is, or if it's another successful match, I put my phone on charge. It's only on 1%. The phone will die before the app even opens. I decide to sleep.

Left

I wash the buttered toast with a swig of apple juice. He's ironing and I make a point of staring.

'So, that's a no then?'

He doesn't lift his head, only his eyes, they pierce through the frames of his thick glasses.

'We said we were done, *you* said we were done.'

I shrug, taking another bite of my toast. Sean shakes his head, turns off the iron and whips his shirt off the board. He begins to button it on.

'Well,' I roll my eyes. 'That's a definite no then.'

'I've gotta get to work otherwise I'll be late.'

'No. It's fine. I get it.'

Turning me down is insulting enough, trying to muster some lame excuse makes my cheeks flush red. Sean pushes the ironing board to the side without collapsing it. I'm sure he does it on purpose to piss me off, he knows I hate it when he leaves it open.

'See, this is exactly why we stopped... you know.'
'What?' I annunciate my words loud and slow. 'Fucking?'
'Jesus, keep your voice down.'
'Why? Everyone knows!' I yell, even though he's walking past me and out the door. 'Everyone knows we slept together!' It seems, only I know, he's deeply ashamed of it.

Super-like

'Oat milk latte with a splash of vanilla syrup for Judith?' The barista says putting my drink onto the table. I hastily thank him, too occupied replying to Michael with the Two Cats.

It's not until I enter my car I realise the barista has left his number on my cup. I try to remember what he looks like as I send him a text.

Left

'I'm definitely not calling him again,' Lilith hums, tucking a strand of her silver hair behind her ear. 'He sweated so much there was a *puddle* on my chest.' She shivers as she recounts the experience.

'I don't mind some sweat,' Kendra whispers. 'Means it's hot and passionate.'

'No Kendra, it means that the man's only form of cardio is missionary for twenty minutes.' Lilith laughs, making no attempt to lower her voice, it echoes across the library. The pair start muttering about the importance of fitness. Lilith makes a point that if women are expected to look fit and healthy, men should make the same attempt. Kendra tries to convince Lilith that either expectation is wrong and unfair.

I remain silent. I've turned my phone off in a desperate attempt to prevent myself from scrolling or more importantly swiping. I'm holding a book in my hands, flicking through the pages, not looking at the words, instead gazing at a couple across the room. They're sat on a plush sofa, engrossed in their books. Every so often the woman fiddles with the tuft of her boyfriend's hair, and he responds by running his hand down her thigh to her knee. It's as though they breathe a little easier when they're touching.

'Jude!' Lilith says, poking my shoulder. 'You never told us what happened with Corey?'

'Not much to say.' I stretch a three-inch gap between my thumb and index finger.

'Oh, that sucks.' Lilith grunts. 'Nothing worse than that.'

Lilith looks at the clock, yanks her jumper off and announces she's going to the café. She does not extend the invitation to either myself or Kendra and we both know why. She wants to meet the new guy who has just started working there.

The couple on the sofa start quietly giggling in each other's ear. Kendra leans over me, grabbing a book in the middle of the table. She becomes a blur in my peripheral vision, but I can tell her gaze has followed mine and landed on the couple.

'They look happy.'

'It'll fade,' I say, flicking another page.

Kendra's olive eyes study my face, 'Maybe.'

A familiar blanket coats me. It's weighted and heavy but not - in the slightest - nurturing. I attempt to shrug it away, trying to focus on the book at hand. The words begin to look like squiggles of ink, so I pull my phone from my pocket and turn it on.

'Or maybe not, you know?' Kendra hums.

I eventually tear my eyes away from my screen, the couple across the library have gone, Kendra has her earphones in and Michael with the Two Cats has asked to see me this evening. The blanket is removed.

Right

I used to swim every day, an hour every evening. For a

long time it felt liberating, sinking my head beneath the water and swimming laps up and down. Then eventually, I became tired, too tired to crawl out of the library or the lecture hall to put on a pair of goggles. But I have made a promise to myself, to feel better and to reintroduce the things that once made me feel warm and light.

The chlorine floods my nose and I inhale deeply. The pool is empty, apart from two elderly women who are hovering in the shallow end, deep in conversation. My bare feet slap against the wet stone as I approach the deep end. The female lifeguard yawns, briefly looks at me, then goes back to inspecting the dirt beneath her fingernails.

The water on my skin is initially cold, but then the temperature rises. With my body on autopilot, I find rhythm and motion, like I never stopped swimming in the first place. I tick off all my little accomplishments of the day: making my bed and having breakfast (not thinking of the run-in with Sean), meeting my deadline and studying all day, going for an evening swim to unwind.

Five laps completed, I pause at the deep end. The pool is now empty, the women have left. It's only me and the lifeguard; she and I are in this together. That's when I realise the female lifeguard is no longer posted.

Aaron, with his leg resting on the other, looks down at me smirking in his red and yellow uniform. He's using his index finger to roll his curly brown hair into a tight ringlet. As my eyes meet his, he wiggles his fingers. I don't want to wave back, but I return the gesture and it's met with a smirk.

I draw my attention back to the water.

The one lap is hard. My breathing is irregular and it's like I'm moving through concrete. A pair of dark eyes watch me, burning onto my back and my arse. I stop at the shallow end. He's still watching, still smirking. My evening swim is over.

A wolf whistle blows through the air like a gust of wind as I unlock my car. Aaron is out of his uniform and wearing a pair of grey joggers and a black hoodie, items I once wore myself.

'Well, as I live and breathe, how are you?' He is laughing, deep dimples sink into his cheeks.

'I'm good thanks, and you?'

This conversation sounds awfully similar to the last conversation we had. A cold shiver vibrates across my skin as he asks about my life and I entertain his questions. The sun has set and, although we're deep into July, I'm wet and tired.

'Sorry, I shouldn't keep you, you should get home.'

He rubs his hand up and down my arm. His fingers were always soft when they touched my skin.

I say it although I know I shouldn't. I have plans with Michael with the Two Cats, but it's a reflex, a habit, like a cigarette after dinner.

'You're more than welcome to come round and hang out for a bit.'

The offer isn't even in the air before Aaron agrees.

Left

He's pulling his boxers on as he's thanking me for the invitation. I turn my back on him and wave goodbye. His face is suddenly inches from mine, trying to kiss my cheek as a formal farewell. I duck my head under the duvet.

'Are... are you okay? he asks.

'I'm fine, just tired.'

It's not a lie, I am tired and heavy. My legs tighten together as I try to ignore the heat radiating between them. I think he has left when I hear a hesitant pull of the door handle and creaking of the floorboard.

'Hey Judith?'

The air is cold as I poke my head out.

'Was the sex... was it good for you?'

'It was.' I'm already trying to forget how his lips glided across my skin. 'I'm just tired.'

He leaves me in my room alone as I pull my phone from

beneath the bundle of clothes. I apologise to Michael with the Two Cats for not replying. I tell him I've been busy. I tell him I would love to rearrange.

Right

It's late when I enter Sean's room.
It's even later when I leave it.

Unmatched

'You said you would stop sleeping with Sean,' Lilith laughs, as I flop onto her unmade bed.
'I know.'
Actually, I said I would stop sleeping with people full stop. I don't care to mention Aaron. Lilith wouldn't judge me, quite the opposite, she would giggle and high-five me, ask me to compare size, girth and stamina. I don't know what I want less, Lilith's enthusiasm or Kendra's judgement.
'Where is Kendra?' I ask.
'I don't know.' Lilith rubs the fake tan into her legs. Kendra isn't usually just on time, she's usually half an hour early. I select her name in my contact list and press call.
'What are you doing? You know she hates phone calls.' Lilith stops bronzing herself and leans her hand on her hip. It's true. We created a group chat and promised each other that we wouldn't phone each other without at least a five-minute warning. I know something is wrong when Kendra picks up on the first dial.

Lilith is driving 60 in a 30 zone, she'll lose her license if caught. She revs to 65. I don't tend to get car sick, and I'm pretty sure I have read somewhere you're less likely to get car sickness in the front seat, yet bile coats my throat and my stomach churns. Kendra's house is on a main road, one where traffic wardens often patrol looking for permits. Lilith doesn't bother indicating when she drives onto the curb outside Kendra's house, switching off the engine.

'You're going to get a ticket.'

'So?' Lilith barks, jumping out of the car. I wait a moment as if looking for upcoming traffic, but in reality, I'm frozen. It doesn't matter if Lilith's caught speeding, or if she gets a parking ticket from a traffic warden. The real problem is only a door away.

I'm sitting at the end of the bed. Lilith and Kendra are entwined in a fluffy blanket and a duvet. It's not particularly cold, the air is still humid and the sun is only just beginning to set, but Kendra is shivering. Her olive eyes have not torn away from the floral pattern on her sheets. Lilith is rocking her side-to-side, her cheek pressed into the thick of Kendra's hair.

'We need to go to the hospital,' Lilith repeats. 'They need to see if you're okay.'

'I've showered now.'

It's true, Lilith and I found her curled on the shower floor with her ripped clothes piled in the corner of the bath.

'It doesn't matter, they still need to check you're okay.'

'They'll call the police.'

That is also true, doctors and nurses have an obligation to report any crime committed. Lilith continues to barter with Kendra. Pins and needles begin to sink into my feet and calves, so I inch away from the pair. A hibernating Mac sits on the desk and as a habit, I move the cursor, activating the computer. It's not password protected and the screen brightens. Her Mac is connected by an HDMI to the TV, which also bursts to life. The dating website is on both the little screen in front of me and the large screen in front of Lilith and Kendra. It shows a conversation:

```
Kendra: Sounds great! My address is 95
Staplefield Drive, BN2 4RH.
```

[read]

It also shows a photo.

'GET HIM OFF THE SCREEN! GET HIM OFF!'

Kendra starts screaming. It makes me jump and I knock a half-empty glass of wine onto the grey carpet. The red liquid spills over my skirt and bare legs. I slam the Mac shut, but it doesn't turn the TV screen off.

'Judith, what the fuck!' Lilith shields Kendra's face in her chest. I stumble over a pile of clothes, trying to reach the cable and yank it out, but I falter. Sound becomes muffled and I'm unable to move. The eyes of Michael with the Two Cats stares right into mine. A notification pings in my back pocket.

The hospital smells of disinfectant. Lilith paces up and down the waiting room and I pull my knees to my chest, hoping that no one will yell at me for having my feet on the chair. Lilith pulls her phone out of her pocket.

'Fuck it, I'm calling her.'

'Lilith...'

She silences me, locating Kendra's mother's name and pressing dial. She storms out of the hospital, leaving me in the empty waiting room. Now and again, I think I hear Kendra's sobs from beyond the ward. It's replaced with the mechanical footsteps of doctors and nurses tracing past me.

The police offer enters the waiting room, looking around. He spots me in the corner, asking if I'm Kendra McCarthy's friend. I should stand, shake his hand like Lilith had done when him and his partner had first arrived, but instead, I nod not moving. He sits beside me, exhaling loudly,

'I know you want to be here for your friend, but there's not much you can do right now. I'd suggest going home, coming back in the morning.' He rubs his eyes, sleep dust hangs on his lower lashes. 'Kendra's making a statement with Officer Wallis, that's all we can do right now.'

I've never personally spoken to a police officer before. I want to tell him I know Michael, Michael with the Two Cats, maybe that could help his investigation, maybe that could help Kendra and her pain. But I can only focus on mine as it radiates through my bones. I burst into an uncontrollable sob.

'It's hard I know,' The police officer sighs, patting me on my back. 'But, you know, you and your friends will have to take this as a lesson.'

The word echoes through me.

'A lesson?'

'Yes, a lesson.' His voice hardens. 'You know, you girls have to be more care-'

I stand, pushing myself out of the chair.

I choke. 'Wi-will you excuse me?'

I await no reply as my numb feet I run out of the waiting room and straight into Lilith.

'Whoa, where are you going?'

I'm pointing behind me, trying to speak through the lump in my throat. My fingers are trembling. I'm unable to catch my breath when I say,

'I've got to go Lilith, *we've* got to go.'

I reach for her handbag, wanting the car keys, but Lilith pulls it away.

'What is *wrong* with you Judith? Our friend has just gone through something horrific and you're running?'

'Lilith...' My fingers are knotting in my hair. 'I've got to—'

Tell you, tell you that I know him.

'Go?' She fishes through her handbag, pulls her car keys out and throws them. The metal clatters by my feet, 'There you go.'

The cold keys burn my fingertips. 'I'm sorry.'

'It's not me you should be apologising to Judith, that could've been us in that hospital bed, either one of us.'

My knees almost buckle. Lilith takes a deep breath in, and then pulls me into a deep hug.

'I'm sorry Judith, it's okay, go home.' Her voice is softer. 'I'll stay here, come back when you can.'

It's 6 a.m. by the time I stumble back into my house. A puff of hot air from an iron radiates from the kitchen. I meet my bedroom door when I feel the blanket looming behind me. It's as though someone with big, overbearing hands is waiting for me to lie down so they can put it over my head. I turn to the door beside mine and push it open.

I ignore the piles of clothes, the food wrappers and the empty cans of alcohol on the floor as I pull the clothes off my body. I crawl onto the mattress, the springs groaning beneath my weight. The room is cold, as is the duvet. I pull my naked body beneath it. I'm barely breathing by the time Sean enters his room.

'Judith?' His voice is slightly stern, before realising I'm swallowing my sobs. 'Judith, what's wrong? What's happened?'

I can't explain what's happened, because I don't know what's happened. I don't know what Michael with the Two Cats did to Kendra. But I know what he has done lingers close, too close. Kendra's name is lost within my cries.

'Can I... Can I touch you?' he asks.

I nod. He pulls me into him.

'I'm going to crease your top,' I say into his crisp shirt, my fingers now clinging onto the lilac material. He tells me not to worry. He again asks me what's wrong. A series of vibrations buzz into the room, I bury my head until Sean mentions that it's my phone.

'Kendra! It might be Kendra!'

'It's okay, I'll get it.' Sean offers.

The worry on his face dissipates as he reads the notification on my phone. It replaced with redness in his cheeks.

'Wow, really Judith?' He holds the phone at arm's distance, squinting to read it. '*Michael's* asking to rearrange your date.' Judgement coats Sean's mouth like slime. 'This is why you're crying? Because some guy stood you up, are you serious?'

'Wait,' I drop the duvet. 'You don't—'

'I thought someone had hurt you Judith, Jesus Christ,' He shakes his head and lowers the phone on the bed. He points to his closed door, 'Please leave, I've got to go to work.'

I want to hug him, tell him he has the wrong idea, but he manoeuvres out of my hold.

'Judith, I can't deal with this... with you right now.' He's not looking at me when he asks, 'Don't you get tired?'

'Tired?'

'Of pretending that sex makes you happy.'

I retract my hands away, his skin scalding my palms. He places my clothes in my arms. I'm stumbling out of the room and before I know it, the door is slammed in my face and I'm stood in the hallway naked.

App Deleted

I know he's left my phone outside my room. It's buzzing on the floorboard on the other side. I do not retrieve it. It can buzz until it explodes for all I care. I lie in bed, with my blinds shut and the TV muttering in the background. I decide to   sleep

POOR VISIBILITY

I

It's raining and sunny at the same time. It makes the air shine like a clementine. I'm dashing out of the car, not bothering with an umbrella. The droplets are large, but surprisingly soft as they land into the thick of my curls and roll down my face.

I'm skipping over a puddle when I spot an elderly woman battling with her bags, trying to lift them into the boot. I beeline towards her, hollering for her to be careful. At first, she doesn't hear me. Then, on the second call, the bag splits. The plastic rips and the contents tumble out, some falling back into the trolley, others onto the sodden floor. I grab a rolling lemon before it is submerged into a puddle that is lined with rainbowed grease. She's exclaiming loudly, flailing her arms above her head. I reach for the tin of biscuits that are caught beside the trolley wheels.

'Here you go,' I lift one of the bags safely into the car. 'Let me help you with the rest.' The woman thanks me, calling me an angel, not even her own son is as kind. 'Oh, I'm sure he is,' I smile, shutting the boot. The sun fades behind a waning cloud; the air shifts grey. She thanks me once again, reaches for my hand, holds it tightly and shakes it up and down. Her skin is warm and wrinkled. She waddles to the driver's seat. My hand is colder than it had been before.

The supermarket is busy. I burst through, my feet following familiar footsteps towards the ready-meal aisle, until the sound of my name echoes. I expect to see someone I recognise. Instead, I am faced with a mother holding tightly onto her crying child, snuggling him close to her chest, reassuring him that everything is okay. The child is bright red in the face, his blond ringlets clamped onto his damp cheeks. When she says our name again, this time softer, the child soothes.

The refrigerated air penetrates my skin as I am faced with

carbonaras, lasagnes, and fish pies. I reach for the cheapest meal, all the while trying to remember the last time someone spoke to me with the same affection.

I'm barely through the door before I'm demanding Alexa to play the radio. The same song I had been listening to on the journey home blasts loudly. I'm reading the instructions on the ready meal as I trail through the living room, dumping my briefcase onto the sofa. It'll take exactly four minutes and thirty seconds in my eight-hundred-watt microwave, or forty-five minutes in the oven. I recite the instructions as if I'm really considering how I am going to cook the meal.

I fling the microwave door open, clearing the previous timer that remains from yesterday and press the new digits in. As the machine whirs to life, I use the time to see if I have any new matches on Tinder. The app opens with no new faces, so I search for a familiar one. Imogen has sent me three new messages and, although I haven't opened them all yet, I spot the most recent.

```
Fancy meeting 2night?
```

I've been sporadically speaking to Imogen for the past five days, out of boredom really. She's eighteen and, even though we have skirted around the topic of our questionable age gap, I imagine she's just some salacious teenager wanting to play out the fantasy of dating a guy in his mid-thirties. I hadn't realised the age setting on the app was so disgustingly low, yet I had swiped on her all the same. Now looking at her profile, where she holds inflatable balloons that spell out 18, and her occupation is titled: student, I suppress a shiver. In the reflection of the illuminated microwave, an old man frowns.

I unmatch her and her profile disappears. I hope that whatever plans she makes for her Friday night are better than mine. I lock the phone, lower it face down onto the counter and watch the numbers on the microwave dwindle. With three minutes and twenty-one seconds to go, I pick up the phone again and start swiping.

I'm hoping the whiskey I poured for dessert will entertain me, but instead, I'm left with a sour tang on the tip of my tongue and a cold, half-eaten dinner laid out in front of me. The few women I have matched with have nothing of value to say, so I click on my contacts list and scroll through, stopping at my brother's name. I haven't heard from him in a while, not since his honeymoon. I command Alexa to silence as Facetime begins to dial. Without the radio playing, heavy droplets of rain ricochet off the windowpane. The sun has fallen and the world outside is dark.

On the eighth dial, I'm about to hang up when the image on the screen morphs into Bradley's pixilated face. There is more beard on him than there is skin. I remember helping him shave for the first time. He shouts out my name, asking how I am before his voice begins glitching on every second syllable.

'Bradley?' I'm squinting as if that will help me figure out where he is, but his screen freezes, showing only his cheek and ear. 'Where are you? I can't hear you... Why have you got shit signal? Bradley?'

I hang up when the camera goes black.

With my top button undone, I wiggle my tie loose and kick my shoes off, reaching for the remote. The TV mutters to life, the weatherman warns the viewers of the heavy storm expected in the next twenty-four hours. He tells us not to leave the house unless it is an absolute necessity. His voice occupies the room as I swirl the rocks in my whiskey glass. In the amber liquid, I see her eyes. I hate associations, they always land on *her*. My index finger is tapping on my phone, all the while I'm trying to convince myself to not message Meghan, that I ought to leave her alone. That neither of us will ever heal with the other still lingering in their life. Why won't I let her heal? Why won't I let myself heal? It's the least we deserve. But I'm unlocking my phone, trying to locate our chat before realising that two weeks ago, in frustration from her last visit, I had deleted our communication. Not her number though, no, never her number. Meghan's photo, although a small oval on the screen, is one I took of her many years ago. Once upon a time, her photo was of us, all three of us.

She was last active almost six hours ago.

```
Bottle of wine with your name on it if
you fancy.
```

It pings off. I swig the remainder of my whiskey, the cold liquid burns my throat. I'm coughing the ache away, catching my breath, when a series of vibrations rattle on my lap. It might not even be her. It might be Bradley apologising for the failed FaceTime earlier, it might be the desolate 'all-lads' group chat bursting back to life. It might even, somehow, be Imogen.

'And I'd just like to reiterate-' The weatherman says in the background, '-there will be poor visibility on the roads so do not leave your house unless it is an absolute emergency.'

```
Will be there in 20.
```

Her long black hair is dripping puddles onto the wooden floor as she trails in front of the lit fire. The storm had caught her as she had dashed from her car into the house. She's fiddling with the ornaments on the mantelpiece whilst nursing a glass of red. She picks up a photo frame of Bradley's wedding and studies it for a moment. It wasn't here the last time she was round. We have managed to avoid the conversation of Bradley's wedding, the one which she had been initially and excitedly invited to. Meghan puts the frame down without saying a word.

'It was a beautiful ceremony.' The words are bursting from my lips, 'Nola looked absolutely beautiful.'

'That doesn't surprise me.' Meghan nods, pursing her lips into a tight line. 'Bradley, how is he?'

'Good,' I nod, approaching her from behind. 'Spoke to him today actually.'

Meghan places her glass of wine on a dusty coaster and

reaches both of her hands out towards the warmth. A shiver rolls through her.

'Let me get you some warm clothes.'

'I'm okay.'

'I insist,' I hold out my hand. 'Come on.'

I wiggle my fingers as she continues to stare at the invitation. She tentatively places her hand into mine. We're not even out of the living room by the time she's peeling away from me.

From the way she walks, a step or two behind me, you'd think she had never lived here before. Her head is slightly dipped, not daring to look into the eye of the place she called home for eight years. Everything looks exactly the same, I haven't changed a thing. Didn't see the point really, replacing what isn't broken. Plus, since she had refused to take anything, not even the damn cutlery she had been hellbent on ordering for our six-year anniversary, it felt like a waste to get rid of anything. Out of the whole house, only one room has been emptied and decorated. Pink paint replaced with clinical white, and all the items stored in the loft, never to be used again. Meghan's feet skip a step as we pass the locked room that still wafts paint fumes.

We step into the bedroom, her usually pale face is blotched pink and red, tears are pricking in her eyes,

'Maybe we should've gone to yours.'

She shakes her head, 'No. I told you last time I didn't want you over.'

Ah, yes, now I remember why I had deleted our chat. Meghan had, as usual, left in a flustered mess and when I proposed the idea to meet at hers next time, she informed me that she never wanted me, or anything that reminded her of me, to step foot in her new flat.

'This is a bad idea,' Meghan murmurs, crossing her arms, standing in the middle of our – *my* – bedroom. She looks small, swallowed by the space around her. I never thought I would describe Meghan that way, not when her laugh always filled up all the empty spaces, not when she always had the knack to put me in my place after a poorly timed, and usually questionably offensive, joke at a dinner party. How could someone with such a sharp and witty tongue be remotely small? She shivers again. I close the gap between us, reaching for the hem of her damp shirt.

'Don't,' I whisper. 'Don't say that.'

It's only when I pull the shirt over her head, that I realise that I do not want to heal. I would rather suffer and struggle. If I do not cling to the pain, the pain will inevitably fade and, if the pain fades, I am left with nothing.

I kiss her. Her erect nipples press against my chest as she wraps her arms around my neck, returning the kiss. A flash of goose-pimples stretch across her cold skin and her lips are soft against mine. I pull her away, staring at the small woman beneath me.

'What?' she whispers, her shaking fingers fumbling at my belt. 'Wh-what's wrong?'

Everything, everything is wrong. I kiss her again, this time harder, drawing her to the bed. I should be more gentle, but I can't stop myself from biting her lower lip. She cries out. When my top is off, her nails dig into my flesh.

ಌ

I bury my head into her neck as I enter her, hoping with all my heart that my tears fall onto the pillow beneath her.

When she climaxes, she turns her head away.

When I climax, I bite my tongue until my mouth is full of blood.

ಌ

I can't believe it. She's asleep, naked, sprawled out under the duvet like she never left in the first place. Her peony lips are slightly parted as she softly inhales and exhales. Almost every light in the house is on. Somewhere in the kitchen, beside a bottle of red wine, my phone is in desperate need of charging. I make no inclination to move. The bulbs can burn and battery can die for all I care. I barely allow myself to shift in the bed, she always was a light sleeper. And, although my eyelids are heavy and beginning to ache, I will myself to stare at Meghan a second longer. The bags under her eyes are puffy and violet. I lower my head to the pillow, sinking into a comfortable darkness quicker than I'd like. I fall asleep thinking that, maybe when I wake up, I'll ask Meghan to marry me.

'WHERE'S THE BLANKET? WHERE'S THE BLANKET?' Her screaming ricochets through me. I'm nearly on my feet, running into the nursery before remembering what reality we are in. I do not have to wake Meghan from the nightmare, her frantic yelling has done the trick. Her warm, olive eyes are wide and her breathing is erratic.

I reach for her, 'It was just a dr—'

No, that's the problem. It wasn't just a dream. For a long time, there is only silence. That is until Meghan says gently, softly, so quietly I almost think I have made it up,

'She has your eyes.'

Meghan exhales loudly as if losing the remaining oxygen in her lungs. She rips her hands out of mine telling me she's got to go. She's on her feet, panting, grabbing her underwear and jeans before I even have the chance to protest.

'Meghan, come back to bed.'

'I regret this… I shouldn't have…'

'Please, don't say that.' My voice begins to shake as I reach for my boxers on the floor. 'You don't regret it, Meghan.'

She stands up tall for the first time in what seems months, stray hairs clinging to her damp cheeks. She's crying, looking straight at me. I stand ready to pull her back to bed, but like an electric shock rippling through the air, she steps back.

'I don't regret coming *here*, I regret *you*.' Her voice is thick, her chest puffing. 'I regret ever meeting you, being with you.'

I turn away. 'You're just upset, you don't mean it.'

'I regret wasting all those years on you, spending all that

time on something that was *always* at breaking point.' She is spitting her words in my direction. 'And I regret, most of all, more than anything, is having Mayla with *you*.'

The words silence the growing storm outside and, despite the nausea churning in my stomach, I will myself to look at her. For the first time since meeting Meghan, I stare at her with indifference. She notices it as she steps forward, whispering my name. Now it is my turn to step back. I collide into the bedside table, the items rattling, some crashing onto the floor by my feet.

'I think you should go,' I murmur, licking the tears that are rolling down my lips. 'You're right, this was a bad idea.'

Meghan, instead of grabbing her shirt, reaches for mine and pulls it over her chest. She's mumbling under her breath as she starts to leave the bedroom and I'm by her heels following her.

As she makes her way down the stairs, I turn towards the closed bedroom door and push it open. Meghan pauses and as I pull it shut, immersing myself in the empty white room, her face removed from sight. I know Meghan wouldn't dare enter Mayla's room, so I lean against the door and slowly roll down until my backside collides on the wooden floor. I press my palms into my wet eyes until I see blue and gold stars dancing amongst the darkness. I try desperately to swallow my sobs. I'm pretty sure, if I listen hard enough, I can hear Mayla's laughter in the rain.

II

Even with my full beams on, I can barely see a few metres ahead. The rain is still heavy and darkness shrouds the roads like a thick blanket. The clock reads 5:06 a.m. I should never have fallen asleep

'Stupid-stupid.' My palms smack against the steering wheel, before my fingers tightly wrap around the curve. My knuckles beaming white. The scent of Kyran's aftershave ignites into the air around my face. I inhale sharply until my lungs are aching and I'm desperate to release my breath. When I do, I scream. Tears blur my vision and I, being the only person on the desolate road, slam on my brakes in the middle of the tarmac. I scream so loud that only Mother Nature and her crushing thunder can drown my cries. Maybe she too can recognise a pain only a Mother would understand.

I curb my old Fiat on the side of the road. It's silly of me really, parking here. There are carparks available across the city, but they're too far away and I'll miss it. I'll miss the sunrise. So instead, I abandon my car on top of two large, recently painted yellow lines that stare at me. I don't care, I can already taste the sea salt on my dry lips.

My feet sink into the pebbles as I run across the empty beach. My calves burn as I try to keep myself from stumbling. The lampposts that line the road are far behind me and ahead - although I can barely make it out through the darkness - is the sea. The water, like the sky, is black. Soon, however, the sun will rise. I plonk myself onto the ground, burying my hands beneath the cold stones and rocks. It is still raining and Kyran's shirt, along with the rest of my feeble clothes, are soaking wet. The weatherman warned about the storm just as Kyran had texted me. I should've heeded his warning but now I'm sitting at the beach, sifting stones through my shaking fingers.

Mayla loved this beach. She loved this beach like I loved this beach as a child, wandering by the shoreline, tipping our wiggling toes into the sea, all the while looking for the perfect pebble to take home or gift to daddy. Mayla always liked the smoothest pebbles the most. I often caught her in her orange floppy sunhat, cross-legged, rubbing stones against her chubby cheeks. I would pull the stone away, only inches from her mouth, fearful of her swallowing it.

'She's not going to swallow it, silly.' Kyran says standing over us, encapsulating us in his shadow from the scorching sun.

POOR VISIBILITY

Mayla is splashing her feet and hands in the shallow sea as I crouch in front of her, holding the black, rounded pebble in my hand.

'What?'

The beach is now crowded and metres away from the shore, I spot Bradley and Nola laughing, playing a game of Uno on a set of towels.

'I said, she won't eat it, silly.' Kyran repeats, bending down and scooping Mayla in his arms. Mayla wraps herself around Kyran's neck and he snuggles her close. The curls by her temple are slightly damp from both sea and sweat, just like Kyran's. Shakily, I stand.

'Will you, peanut?' He coos and Mayla giggles. I reach out, my fingers grazing her soft cheeks. She stares at Kyran with her large, amber-doe eyes.

'Are you okay?' Kyran asks, moving wet hair away from my eyes and tucking it behind my ears. 'What's wrong?'

'I'm sorry.' I gasp, my teeth chattering. 'I didn't mean what I said.' I step into Kyran's embrace, my face nuzzling into Mayla's warm belly. 'I don't regret this. I don't regret this one bit.'

'I know,' Kyran soothes. 'I know you don't.'

There is so much on the tip of my tongue, but I am unable to speak. My skin and body numb. I am engulfed by the bustling beach and squawking seagulls. I want to tell Kyran that I love him and I always will, but I don't know what to do with the excess love I have stored within me, within my womb. The love I have for Mayla has nowhere to go and I'm drowning within it. I want to tell him I come over every time he asks, knowing we'll inevitably have sex and I secretly pray that I will again fall pregnant. Yet afterwards, I am consumed with a debilitating sickness, feeling as though I am trying to replace Mayla just so I can get rid of the love inside of me. Even with all of this unsaid, Kyran reaches his warm hand out to caress my cheek. He opens his mouth, but it is not his voice when he says,

'Wake the fuck up gal!'

POOR VISIBILITY

The air is grey again, but lighter than before. The beach is empty and delicate droplets of rain are falling all around me. A man, dressed head-to-toe in khaki green is bent over me. He stinks of piss and his beard is inches away from my face.

'You're asking for death to pay ya a visit lying in the cold'n'wet like that!' His Irish accent is thick. 'What do ya think you're doin?'

'I-I-' I sit upright, wiping the rain and tears from my eyes. 'I wanted to watch the sunrise.'

'In a fookin' storm?' he retorts. Behind the clouds somewhere, the sun has already risen. 'Go home gal.' He extends a hand to me and gingerly, I accept his help. Salt tingles my skin and my legs shake like jelly when I stand. I kick my feet through the pebbles as I walk back to the car, noticing a black shiny, round pebble protruding out amongst the rest. I reach down to pick it up.

I inspect the stone as I walk away from the sea and back to my Fiat. Only until I've pulled the parking ticket from my windshield, put the key in the ignition and whacked the heating up, I bring the pebble to my face. I rub it against my cheeks. This time when I cry, I hear Mayla's laughter in the crashing of the sea.

STRANGERS EVERYWHERE

The aroma of coffee beans is so strong it punctures my nostrils and I almost turn and leave. The cafè is busy, something I have rarely seen, not since the start of COVID-19. It's not the anxiety of the disease that makes me want to leave, it's her, as she sits in the corner on the plush sofa. Her back is to me but I know it is her with her burgundy hair, styled in loose waves that arch down her spine. I remember how it felt when she was a little girl asking – no, begging me to plait it. Leaving would be easy. I could use Zane as an excuse, maybe pick him up earlier from his playdate at Frannie's.

'Umm, excuse me.' A large pushchair edges close to me. 'Could you—?' The mother points to the door behind me. I hold it open and the little girl coos at me and the mother thanks me.

'You're welcome.'

My voice seems to carry through the bustling café as Lucy's eyes fixate on me. A faint smile etches across her face, but it doesn't quite meet her eyes. She wiggles her fingers over her shoulder, and then with the same hand, beckons me over. Too late to leave now, I make my way toward my baby sister.

She is not a baby anymore, not as she towers over me and embraces me into a tight hug. Her skin is seasoned with cinnamon and apples, and I am immersed in autumn. I wonder if she can smell baby sick on mine. I sit opposite a ghost with her rain-cloud eyes and sporadic freckles. She fidgets, crossing her leg one way and then another, placing her hands in between the crevice of her thighs.

'You look well Els, really well.'

She's lying, I look like shit. I haven't slept in two years or gone to the gym in five.

'Thank you,' I smile although the nickname makes my stomach tight. 'You look lovely, Lucy.' The coffee machine bursts to life and I motion to the queue. 'What do you want?'

'No need.' Lucy holds up her phone and Order 13 flashes on her screen. Without my contacts in I can't read the fine print, especially as she continues to wiggle the phone side-to-side.

'Decaf cappuccino with oat milk?' I say with a false glimmer of hope in my throat.

'Oh,' Her face falls as does the phone in her hand. 'I'll-I'll try and change it.'

'Here you go!' a chippy voice says, lowering two white mugs on the table. One has a teabag floating in delicate pink water, emitting a warm scent of raspberry and elderflower. The other, a harsh black americano.

'I'm sorry,' Lucy reaches for the americano. 'I'll have this and you can have mine.'

'No-no, it's fine.' She's already holding it. 'No honestly Lucy, I won't drink that.' I push the fruity tea in her direction. I won't drink the americano either, but one of us might as well enjoy this spontaneous reunion. She takes the mug and her fingers pinch the teabag string. She stares into the liquid as if it were a magic ball and she is trying to see how this meeting will go. She should know, she called me. A baby wails in the background and Lucy uses this opportunity to ask about Zane. Maybe it's because of the crying child, maybe it's because of the incorrect order, maybe it's because I'm sitting opposite a stranger I call a sister, I ignore her query about my son.

'Lucy,' I shake my head. 'Why am I here?'

I remember the first time I ever laid a hand on Lucy. My palm collided with her cheek, and the sound echoed into the quiet, desolate house. She collapsed onto the sofa, piled with blankets and cushions that I once used to hold her as a baby. I slapped her because our mother always said it taught important lessons like when not to talk back, when we should be seen not heard, when we should have gotten better grades. I can't remember what lesson I was trying to teach Lucy by employing our mother's methods, but I do recall the moment of realisation that it was totally and utterly wrong.

Making her cry like a feral animal taught her nothing of value. I wanted to tell her I was sorry, instead, I told her to stand up and stop crying. I wiped her tears using the same hand I had slapped her with, noticing the sting on my palm and the swollen lines imprinted by her eyes. It wasn't until she apologised for me hitting her, I despised myself.

'I'm sorry Els, I'm really sorry.'

She says it now with tears welling in her eyes and the look of utter shame flooding her cheeks. I remind myself that I am not my mother. Instead, I am quiet and still. My body melting into the chair beneath me. A deep, monotonous hum vibrates in my ears, and I can only make out Lucy's apologies.

'I-I-' My mouth is disgustingly dry, so I reach for the americano. I take a hearty swig, downing it all in one gulp before realising it's scalding hot. My phone vibrates and although my hands are shaking, the respite from staring at Lucy will ease the erratic beating of my heart, that is until I see the caller I.D. The photo of our honeymoon decorates the screen. Like my son throwing a temper tantrum, I hurl the phone and it thumps beside Lucy's feet. I'm out of my chair, running, ignoring Lucy call my name.

The toilet floor is damp and sodden, my fingernails scraping against the tiles. Lucy is outside, demanding the manager use the master key to open the door. I cannot bear to hear the fuss anymore, so I unlock it. As it swings open, Lucy pushes her way through and shuts it in the manager's face. She stands over me,

'Els—'

'I am *not* Els!' I grit my teeth. 'I haven't been for years, not that you would know. You do not know anything about me, not anymore.' How could she? Here sits a woman lost in a sea of mortgage and diapers, of late nights with a child who refuses to sleep with anyone but me. Lucy nestles herself beside me. I should be far away from her, retching from her touch, but as my head falls onto her shoulder, sobbing, I realise there is no one else I want to console me from the pain radiating from my stomach, even if it was planted there by her.

'I never meant for it to happen, Els-*llie*, it was a mistake.'

I bite on my lower lip until the gum bleeds. 'He doesn't know you're telling me, does he?' I swallow the metallic tang. Lucy shakes her head. No, of course he doesn't. He wouldn't have kissed me before he left for work this morning. He wouldn't have smiled sweetly, telling me to have a good day. She invited me last minute. He's clueless.

'I know Zane has a playdate on Tuesdays.'

'How do you—?' The creases in my face soften. 'So, this has been going on for a while then?'

'It's stopped now.' Her cold eyes glance down. 'It started during lockdown.'

'Lockdown? But he's a key worker...'

My hero. The *country's* hero. Where, on Tuesdays at seven o'clock, the street and the entire United Kingdom clapped for people like my husband and his service. I guess an hour later, on his supposed shift, he was fucking my sister. No greater thank you than that, is there? I narrowly miss the toilet as I throw up the americano. It's still burning hot as it travels up my throat and out my mouth.

The world had started to panic and no one had a clue about how to proceed with COVID-19. The economy was put on standstill, masks became as important as toilet roll and there was even a suggestion to guzzle bleach. My husband mentioned how he had bumped into Lucy in a queue for Tesco. It was the first time I had heard of or thought of my sister in a very long time.

'She's moved to Maidenhead now,' Andy said kicking off his slippers. 'She's going to be locked down in her apartment alone.'

It was a rarity that Andy and I were in the house at the same time, let alone getting into bed together. I was elated, watching him perch on the edge of the bed, pulling off the watch I bought him for our wedding anniversary.

'She told me she tried texting you.'

He eventually joined me beneath the covers and I shifted myself close to him.

'She's lying.'

'She said you never replied.'

'More lies.'

I lifted my leg over his.

'Well, she gave me her number to give to you just in case you lost—'

My hands travelled down his boxers, asking,

'Andy, why are we talking about *Lucy* right now?'

I wonder if he thought of her that night when we made love.

I wipe the vomit from my chin and splash my face with tepid water as Lucy explains it never became physical, until two days ago when he had kissed her and slipped his hand between her legs.

'Stop!' I demand, silencing her. From the reflection of the stained mirror, her mouth tightens. 'It doesn't matter anyway.' I breathe. 'I don't care if he fucked you or not, it's irrelevant. Affairs begin long before there is anyone to have an affair with.' My heart aches. 'An affair doesn't start with another person, it starts when the relationship crumbles.' I try to still my quivering lip. 'It starts when a conversation in the kitchen three summers ago dissolves into disappointment.' My voice softens. 'It starts when there is silence at the dinner table or a sulk in the taxi ride home.'

'What is your problem? Seriously!' he slammed the taxi door a little too hard making me flinch. It wasn't even midnight and we were leaving the Christmas party. I ripped the blue tinsel out of my hair, dropping it in the footwell. The taxi man asked for the postcode only until Andy settled into the back beside me.

'What happened Eleanor?'

'Don't call me that!'

'I thought you were having a nice conversation with Pam

and Dave?'

I looked at the dark sky, 'They just spoke about their kids the whole time.'

'Oh, my love.' Andy cooed, his voice now gentle. 'I know we've been trying for a while, but it will happen when the time is right.' His fingers searched for mine and I jerked away. The stars blurring through my tears. I did not cry because of our failure to conceive. It was during that conversation with Pam and Dave, I realised that I was grateful that I had not fallen pregnant and that maybe, *just maybe*, I didn't want kids at all. That night we slept in separate rooms. A week later I found out I was pregnant with Zane.

We're sitting beside each other, Lucy's fingers entwined with mine when a series of violent knocks vibrate through the bathroom door.

'I'm sorry but if you don't vacate in the next five minutes, we're going to have to call the police.' I am the first to peel away from the bathroom floor and, as I stand over her, I offer her a hand. We exit together.

A small crowd of baristas hovering by the door, wanting to see who caused the commotion. It seems they are disappointed to see two sad, lost sisters emerge out of hiding.

'Here you go,' a scrawny man with the name badge Peter hands me my phone. 'It's been going crazy since you locked yourself in there.'

'It's not the only thing going crazy,' I reply, taking the phone. Peter tells me to look after myself. I think that's his way of saying he forgives me for locking myself in the bathroom. I have five missed calls from Frannie and twelve from Andy. Glancing at the time, it turns out Lucy and I have been hibernating for almost three hours.

```
Frannie called me, why didn't u pick up Zane?
Had 2 leave work 4 this.
Are u okay? What is going on?
Where are you?
This is ridiculous - call me!
```

The air is heavy, thick grey clouds line the sky. A few buildings away, however, there are clear skies ahead.

'Is that him?' Lucy points to my locked screen, a photo of Zane smiling.

'Yeah, that's him.'

'He looks like you.' Her eyes do not pull away from my phone even when it darkens. 'I'll see you around?'

'Probably not.'

'No, yeah… fair enough.' She looks over her shoulder towards the car park. 'Bye Els.' She pulls me into a hug.

I pat her on the back, returning the squeeze. I think of all the things I could tell her, like I'm sorry I hit you when we were kids, I'm sorry I didn't protect you from mum, I'm sorry we weren't there for each other when things got tough. Instead, in the thick of her burgundy hair, I whisper,

'I forgive you.'

I let go and turn away, her soft cries carrying in the wind.

GOLDEN

Dreaming

He's by my side when my heavy eyes flutter awake, of course he is. Where else would he be? The sun is rising beyond the closed window and the room, even against the clinical grey and white, looks warm. Jonathan's eyes flicker as he looks down at our wedding band on his finger. It's not as bright as it once was. His hand squeezes mine.

'Jonathan,' my voice no longer sounds like it belongs to me, so I'm not surprised to see him flinch. He inches towards the cup of untouched water and I slowly shake my head.

'Lana.' Jonathan's voice breaks. The lines by his eyes are deeper than I remember and his beard longer. His eyes pierce mine and even though the room is light, soft, golden, they darken and then he bursts into tears. His head rests in my lap. My fingers reach the tuft of his thick hair, his sobs echoing through me. At least I will never know a world without him.

Lucid

I finally vacate the room, Melanie stands from the chair she had wrapped herself in. Her husband, Nathan, stands like a bulldog by her side.

'Did she think you two were—'

'Yes.' My voice is harder than I intend it to be. 'Yeah, she did. I let her think it was real.' Melanie embraces me and I return the hug as she starts crying in my arms.

'Go in there,' I say, rubbing her back. 'She might wake up again.'

Although muffled in the crease of my hoodie, I hear her clearly,

'No, she won't.'

I close my eyes, hot tears spilling down my face. I find the strength and pry myself out of Melanie's grip.

'I've gotta' go Mel, I'm sorry.'

'What you did for Lana—'

'Don't mention it.' I plead. I don't look back at the hospice door as I leave. Gravity will pull me back to her. I can't say goodbye for the third time.

I burst out of the building and catch my breath, the cold air biting my skin. A young woman sitting on a brick wall puffs on a cigarette. Her face is red, eyes swollen and tears stain her cheeks.

'Want one?' She offers, tugging at the woollen hat on her head.

'I shouldn't.'

'That's not a no.' She extends the packet out to me. I take a cigarette, using her lighter to ignite the tobacco. I take a long and painful drag on the cigarette, perching beside her.

'So, who is it?' She gestures to the building behind us. 'Mum? Brother? Child?'

'Wife.' As the word escapes my lips I am on my feet, pacing down the steps.

'Wait! I'm sorry! I didn't mean to—'

But I'm already reaching the car park, her voice fading amongst the waking city.

I walk down the garden path when my phone vibrates in my pocket. I know what it's going to say when Melanie's name occupies my screen. But even when I read the words: She's gone, I almost buckle on my doorstep. I'm given no time to catch my breath when the door swings open.

'Ah, shit!' Chloe jumps. 'There you are!' She's dressed in her most expensive, navy suit. Her honey hair is in a lopsided bun, half-eaten toast in one hand. 'Where did you run off to this morning? I've been calling you all—'

'Daddy! Daddy!' Lily charges through Chloe's legs and throws herself into me. I catch her, lifting her into the air before tightening her into my arms. 'Mummy's been angry at you *all* morning!' Lily's fingers poke at my beard. 'She called you names like little ARSEHOLE.'

'Lily!' Chloe scorns before I even have the chance to. 'Go put your tights on, you're going to be late for school.'

I enter the house, scooting Lily up the stairs to get ready. Chloe, continuing to moan, takes a deep breath in. Her button nose tightens and lines crease on her face.

'Wow, really? You nearly made me late for work because you couldn't beat a craving?' She shoves the cold piece of toast into my hand and pulls at her hair to redo it. 'Lily, hurry up! Daddy's taking you to school.'

When Chloe revealed she was pregnant with Lily, after only one month of us dating, I felt three emotions. Pride, that the fertility issues between myself and Lana were not because of me. Smug, that my swimmers were capable of doing the very thing they're supposed to do. Then came the overwhelming guilt. I was unable to give Lana the very gift I had without meaning to, without wanting to, given to Chloe. Eventually, over the course of a tough nine months and a traumatic birth, it didn't take me long to realise it was Chloe who had gifted me Lily. Lily, who is now sitting in the backseat on the way to primary school, giving me a gift: the gift of distraction.

'Did you know that Daddy?'

'Did I know what?'

In the rear-view mirror, Lily rolls her eyes the same way her mother had done this morning. 'We had to pick an animal to research in the library and I chose—'

'Elephant!' We say together. She squeals. Ellie the Elephant has always been her favourite. 'And did you know Daddy that elephants are the only animal in the world that can die from a broken heart?' It's going to be a cruel day when Lily discovers that is simply not true. A day that, despite my best efforts, I know I cannot prevent.

Chloe's car is gone by the time I'm back. In our bedroom, she laid my work clothes on the bed with a note, telling me my lunch is in the fridge. I'm rushing to get ready, knowing

GOLDEN

I'm going to be late when the doorbell rings. I recognise the outline beyond the door, but I'm confused as to why my boss is on my doorstep. That is until I swing the door open and the only word that exhales from Jax's lips is,

'Mate.'

In the midst of our divorce, Lana sent me an ill-advised article on how to get through a tough breakup. The title had been printed in some fancy font and the article was nearly five pages long, front and back. The first bullet point encouraged the divorcee, in this case the both of us, to rely on *'Your Support System: See friends, family, loved ones'*. It suggested cramming as many people as you possibly could into one day and being surrounded by *'good vibes'*. What this article didn't tell you is that your loved ones start looking at you a little differently. They look at you the same way Jax is looking at me right now, heavy and solemn. Of course he is, his wife was a good friend of Lana's.

I invite him in before he gives me the 'I'm sorry' speech on my doorstep. I direct him into the living room, scooping Lily's Barbies out of the way, mounting them into a pile.

'I wanted to come here and personally offer my condolences,' Jax says. 'And to tell you to take the day off.'

'No, I don't need—'

The shaking of Jax's head silences me, 'Jon, take the day off. Melanie told Janine what you did this morning.' What I did at 4 a.m. this morning is none of his business, let alone hearing the series of events through the grapevine. Jax shifts on his chair and folds his hands into his lap, chewing on the bottom of his lip. He didn't come here for my pain, he came here for his. I can't help myself from asking, through gritted teeth,

'How long did you know? How long did you know she was terminal?'

For a long time, I struggled to be around Jax. He was a direct link between my old life and my new life. It became an unspoken rule to never mention Lana around me. That was until, when enough time had passed, I could utter Lana's name on the tip of my tongue without feeling like I would double over in pain. The first time, and the last time, I asked about Lana was two months ago.

So, how's Lana doing?

The question had made his face tight. I believed it was because Lana had become a foreign entity between us. His words still echo,

Yeah, fine mate. Doing well I believe.

'Jon, I wanted to tell you.' He now informs me, his eyes looking into his lap. 'I mean, I assumed initially you knew from social media, but when I realised you didn't— shit man, Janine told me not to get involved.'

It has been years since I searched for Lana on social media. The last time I had was nearly three years ago. Lily was asleep in our bed with Chloe and I was nursing a bottle of gin, celebrating what would technically have been our fifteenth anniversary. I had been up until 5 a.m., zooming into photos of Lana travelling the world, visiting art exhibitions, skiing in the alps; living the life I always dreamt of. It wasn't until I realised, with a successful marriage and a healthy child, I was living the life she always dreamt of. I blocked her that night.

I muster the courage to ask Jax, who is still silent, to leave. I don't let myself cry until the front door is shut.

It takes me a while to find the key. We had purposefully hidden it to prevent Lily from finding it. When I do, I'm standing on the third floor at the top of the stairs, unlocking the loft door. After a series of jiggles and twists, it finally opens, and a gust of cold air carries through my clothes. It doesn't take me long to locate it: *'The Suitcase of Shit'*. I had told Chloe that it contained memorabilia from my younger years. I guess she had forgotten that all my younger years, from the ripe age of fourteen, contained Lana. It's loosely hidden behind a pile of Chloe's University tuition books.

Ready to face nearly twenty years of memories, I pull it from its hiding place. It's lighter than I remember and when I open it, I find only a handful of items. The album is lying on top and a layer of dust coats my fingers as I pry it out. Before

I even have time to investigate it, the front door slams, making me jump and the photo album tumbles from my fingers. The dust disperses around me and the album opens on a photo of Lana. She's on her knees in her sunflower dungarees, holding a paintbrush. We were decorating our old house. If I try hard enough, I can smell the paint. It is effortless, however, to hear the echoing of her laughter.

'Jon!' Chloe calls.' Are you home?'

I gently close the album shut, placing it on top of the suitcase. The camera did not do Lana justice, it did not pick up her forest green eyes or the mole beneath her brow.

'What are you doing in here?' The sound of Chloe's voice in the loft takes me by surprise. She's stood under the arch, her jacket hanging in her arms and her blouse unbuttoned revealing her black laced bra. Her light hair, now completely untamed from the bun, sways by her shoulders. 'Why aren't you at work?' Her eyes glance at the album. 'What's that?'

I approach her, her mouth gaping open ready to ask another question. I grab her waist and pull her body into mine, placing my lips on hers whilst doing so. I can't remember the last time we had sex, months ago maybe, probably in the dark with our socks on, trying not to disturb Lily in the next room. When I first met Chloe, in the midst of my crumbling relationship with Lana, I took solace in Chloe's body. I yearned for her touch, her skin. As a young woman, over a decade younger, Chloe responded to every touch. A bit like now, as she wraps her legs around me, her fingers running through my hair, moans escaping her lips as my tongue explores her neck. I fall into Chloe as I had done six years ago, desperate and lost.

I wake up and the bed is empty. The sheets are in a tangled mess, uprooted from the mattress, dangling on the floor. Both of our clothes are strewn across the room, my boxers however in reaching distance. The door is ajar and, as I creep out into the hall, I hear the rummaging of items echo from the attic. I know what she's doing before I see her.

In her fluffy dressing gown, she's sat crossed-legged on

the loft floor with the photo album perched on her lap, opened. She's holding the ring box that contains my old wedding band.

'Is this where you were this morning?' Chloe asks, not lifting her head. 'With her?'

'Yes.'

She exhales heavily, as if winded. 'It was always going to happen.'

'Chloe, you don't understand—'

'You know a month after we started dating, I ran into your mother.' Chloe continues to examine the ring. 'She spotted me at the market, must've recognised me from a photo you showed her or something. She told me I was wasting my time.' She finally meets my gaze. 'She told me it was always Lana. That it always was and always will be, Lana. I should save myself the heartache and leave now, but it was too late, I was pregnant.

'She was right, wasn't she? It'll always be Lana, won't it?' Chloe lowers the box, tears spilling from her eyes, her fingers tracing the album. The sun pierces through the window, reflecting off the plastic film, hiding all the photos from my eye. I'm thankful. They say you cannot lie to a lawyer, that they'll always know the truth by the flicker of expression. But, in honesty, you can lie to anyone when they're desperate enough to hear a particular answer.

'No, no it won't,' I shake my head. 'Chloe, I was with Lana but not in the way you think.'

Our eyes firmly stare into the cup of tea perched in front of us. When we do finally look up, the clock slowly approaching three, we both murmur Lily's name in harmony.

'I'll go,' she says.

'Thanks.'

'Will you go to the funeral?' Without even a moment's pause, she adds. 'Silly question, of course you will.'

Lana and I, after a bottle of red wine and our bellies full of cheese and crackers, often spoke about death. We discussed our funeral arrangements; elaborated on how we intended to leave this world. However, that was a long time ago now. The arrangements we made at eighteen, twenty-four or even thirty would not be the same.

'I don't know,' I admit. 'I don't what I'm doing.'

Chloe reaches for my hand and caresses it. In a whisper, she tells me that I'm a good person, that whatever I decide will be the right thing, that what I did this morning made me the kindest man she ever knew. I am fortunate when Chloe announces she's leaving to get Lily.

'When I'm back, I'll make us a nice dinner, okay?' Chloe kisses my cheek.

'Sounds lovely,' I say, despite knowing full well I have no intentions of being here when she gets back.

Phone dead, pub shut, I stumble down the pavement ready to make my way home. However, when I stand on a doorstep, nearly tripping over the 'WELCOME HOME' mat, I'm surprised to find myself banging on the front door, which is opened by Nathan in his dressing gown frowning down at me.

'Is Mel—?' I hiccup.

Melanie ushers herself in front of her husband, also in a dressing gown. She rests her hand on Nathan's chest telling him to go to bed, that she'll take care of me. Shit, I need to be taken care of?

'Should I go?' I point behind me into the darkness. I don't even remember the sun setting.

'No, no.' Melanie reaches for my hand, gently pulling me in. Her hand is warm and she directs me through the house. My footsteps retrace themselves. They have wandered through this hall many times, for gatherings, pizza nights and game nights. We enter the living room where a thick duvet occupies the sofa.

'I've been sleeping down here for a while, can't seem to settle in my bed.' Melanie folds the duvet into the corner. The TV is on but muted. It's the only source of light, that is until Melanie clicks a lamp on. As my eyes adjust to the brightness, the photo of Lana on the wall illuminates. It's the photo I took of both of them on the day of Lana's graduation. As twin sisters, most people think they're identical in every way but I never thought so. Lana's sparkle was always brighter. Melanie's hand rests on my shoulder, reminding me where I am.

'Sit down Jon.' I do as I'm told and the room begins to spin. I apologise as my head falls into my palm. She rubs my back, 'It's me who should be saying sorry.' Tears spill down her cheeks. 'Asking you to see her... but she was *adamant* Jon, she wanted you not me. I just couldn't tell her that you weren't together anymore...Jesus, asking anyone to do what I asked you to do would—'

Haunt them.

'I'd do it all again you know, for her.'

'I know.'

'Why didn't she tell me? When she found out?' The look in Melanie's eyes cuts through me and I too start crying. 'I would've taken care of her, if she let me. I would've helped her.' My nose runs and I wipe it with the back of my hand, but I'm unable to stop myself when I tell Melanie that, even after all this time, I love Lana. Melanie wraps her arms around me so tightly, it's as if she is trying to put me back together. I howl so loud that I hope wherever Lana is, she hears me, that she knows, despite it all, I am connected to her as we had been at fourteen, as we should've been in life.

I wake up, dribble staining my chin. A duvet is over my clothed body and Melanie, curled up in the armchair, has only a measly blanket over her thin body. The light and TV are off. From beyond the closed curtain the world is beginning to wake up. Delicate sunrays pierce through the gaps. Melanie is awake and from the bags under her eyes, it doesn't look as if she has slept. She is staring at the graduation photo. I straighten up, an intense thump vibrates through my skull. I try to coat my cracked lips with saliva when Melanie motions towards the glass of water on the table. I grab it, noticing the envelope on her lap. I recognise the handwriting.

GOLDEN

Jon

'Tell me that isn't—'

'Oh, but it is.' Melanie confirms, her fingers running along the edges. 'Please don't tell me to get rid of it, I can't defy any more of her wishes than I already have.'

'What do you mean?' The water softens my voice and the ache in my head. Melanie leans forward, the blanket falling into her lap.

'You'll find out.' She extends the envelope. 'Take it.'

❧

It's raining outside as I write this, I'm glad. I've always loved the smell of the rain, just like you've always loved the feeling of the sun on your skin. I'm also glad I'm writing this when I'm well enough because I know soon, I will not be able to. Some days are worse than others. It turns out you lose all pride and dignity when you're dying. It also turns out, it doesn't really matter. Some days are better, the best days however are when I still believe I am married to you.

It's a bit like lucid dreaming really, but halfway through the lucid dream, I forget only to remember later. I like the bit where I forget it is a dream. I think soon, if I'm lucky, I will forget entirely. However, right now, I'm lucid enough to remember you are my ex: ex-husband, ex-lover, ex-best friend.

I have told Mel that under no circumstances are you to see me when I am dreaming. No matter how many times I ask when my 'husband' will be coming to see me.

GOLDEN

It wouldn't be fair to pull you back into a timeline we have both said farewell to. And, from what I hear, you have bigger things – or one rather small, adorable thing – to look after now. When you're dying you think of all the experiences you missed out on. I still think hearing our child call you 'daddy' will be one of the biggest for me.

As I am on my deathbed, I want to let you know that there is no other way I'd like to go, except wildly and passionately in love with you. It was the only time I truly felt alive.

I always thought, in some way, we'd find each other again. If it will not be in this lifetime Jonathan, I fucking hope it's the next. That, when we get another chance, we do it right. I used to tell myself, in the heat of our divorce, there was a reason why we had to leave each other. God feared what we had. Stumbling into your arms as I did in year 9 chemistry threatened the very balance God created – complacency. We were many things Jonathan, but complacent was not one.

Isn't it telling? Even as I'm moving from this world to the next, there is something tethering me back to you. The doctors say it's a symptom of the disease, I think it's God's failure to keep us apart. Not even death can separate us. It's a shame life certainly tried.

I love you.
Yours. Always.
Lana x

GOLDEN

The loft door is ajar and the key is still in the lock. I push it open, the hinges creaking. In the centre of the room, the photo album and ring box are perched on top of the suitcase. I kneel in front of it, my aching bones resting on the wooden floor. I move the items off the case and pull Lana's letter out of my back pocket. I bring the paper to my nose and inhale deeply, hoping to smell remnants of her. Instead, I can only detect the faint trace of ink. In the suitcase, I place the album, the ring box and finally the letter.

Sometimes magical things happen, like when it's sunny and raining at the same time, as it is now. The rays pierce through the attic whilst large thick droplets pitter-patter against the window. My nose is filled with the scent of dry pavement and grass becoming damp, my skin illuminating, the air stretching golden. I zip the suitcase shut.

I walk out of the loft, pulling the door close, leaving the key in the lock untouched

THUNDER ONLY HAPPENS WHEN IT'S RAINING

'You were right, okay?' I whisper. 'I bet you love hearing that, don't you?'

Rain droplets roll down her gravestone and ants scatter to find shelter in the earth. The weather had predicted overcast with no rain, I guess they made a mistake too. The rain begins to fall heavier and the cold water finds its way down the collar of my shirt, rolling across my goose-pimpled skin. All my clothes have gotten far too big recently. I blow a kiss to my mother, all the while considering staying at the grave a moment longer, a bit of rain never hurt anybody. Lightning flashes above my head. I guess I can't avoid home forever.

I twist the key so softly I hope he doesn't hear me, but he's walking down the stairs as I swing the door open. Another flash of lightning pushes its way into the house.

'Jeez, it's miserable out there.' His gaze shifts to my face. 'Where have you been?'

'The grave.' I don't mention the two detours I took to get home. He doesn't kiss me as he walks past. Instead, he hollers over his shoulder that my dinner is in the oven. It's a Tuesday, I bet it's lasagne.

'It's lasagne.' He says from the living room as the TV mumbles to life. I don't know what I want to do more, laugh or cry. I tell him I'll eat later and head upstairs to draw a bath.

I can't remember when I started locking the bathroom door. When we were newly married, I'd leave the door ajar so he'd follow me into the shower. Francis always got the message then. It seems he still does because he leaves me well alone. Fleetwood Mac blasts from the speaker as I lower myself into the tub. The song is not even into the chorus when I start uncontrollably sobbing. If I eat lasagne again, I will vomit. The music isn't loud enough to drown my cries, so I lower my head beneath the bubbles to scream.

When my lungs are aching for oxygen, I lift my head out of the water. My heavy, wet hair drags past my ears. Although the room is full of steam, I spot the sink tap leaking. Thankfully, I cannot hear the water dripping onto the porcelain. This will be Francis's fourth, maybe fifth, attempt to fix the tap. I told him to get a professional, knowing his handiwork wouldn't be up to par. He had insisted otherwise. I tried to change his mind, but he got upset, so I dropped it. We haven't spoken about it since, and our tap is still broken.

The knock on the bathroom door jolts me.

'I just wanted to let you know I'm going to bed, I've dished your dinner and put it in the fridge.' I reach for my phone. I've been hiding in the bathroom for almost an hour. 'Try and eat tonight Kathy, even if it's a little bit.'

Not even the wooden door between us can hide his solemn and rounded eyes. I see it in everyone these days when they look at me. They look at me like I am fading. At first, they admired it, how my slim figure complimented my smile and eyes. Now both features are too large for my sinking face.

'Will do, I'm just getting out now.'

He tells me not to rush, so I wait until his footsteps are down the hall and into our bedroom before unplugging the bath. The water begins to twirl down the drain. It gurgles until the tub is empty.

I crawl into the bed. I stay on my side and Francis, dutifully, stays on his. The small distance between us feels so uncomfortably large, I daren't cross it. A threshold I am not welcomed into. A strip of light from the lamppost outside stretches across the room illuminating Francis's back. He forgot to shut the curtains before falling into bed. I feel no inclination to move. Instead, I study the arch of his back, remembering a time when my fingers would trail down each vertebrae. Like a piece of a puzzle wanting to fit, I will myself to reach out and touch him. His skin, in comparison to mine, is burning hot as my bony fingers move against his flesh. My touch startles him and he mumbles my name. As he turns to face me, it is my turn to be startled. The stretch of light reveals the grey hairs that have been painted like brushstrokes within his dark hair. The wrinkles by his sleepy eyes remind me that it was long ago when I first studied his curling spine and found a home. He is not eighteen anymore, and when he gently pulls me into him, his lips finding mine, I realise neither am I. I am not the teenager who had said 'I do' despite her mother's dismay.

The lamppost switches off and we are immersed in darkness. I want nothing more than to fall asleep, but I return the kiss. I do not object when his hand runs up my thigh. Maybe he too is trying to find what we lost. Maybe he is also wondering how time had moved and moulded us into … this.

I sleep with him. It's what you're supposed to do when you're married. I'm just happy that he doesn't notice the tears when he's on top of me. Grateful that even if he does, he says nothing.

⚡

I dream of my mother. Her small, rounded stature with a cigarette in one hand and an old charity-bought book in the other. She is sitting on the patio doorstep, overlooking the unkept garden and the falling crimson leaves. I take my place beside her.

'I hated you.' My voice is cold, distant. It belongs to the past. 'I hated that you made me choose.' I've heard these words before, so when she replies with only a soft shake of her head, I am not surprised.

'You do not hate me for making you choose.' Her voice is thick as if a ventilator is attached to her nose. 'You hate yourself for choosing him.'

We turn to face each other, she is no longer the young

plump mother sitting in her dressing gown. She's old and thin, her skin sagging. Her bones brittle from the cancer that has eaten her alive. She reaches out to touch my hand. Both of our fingers as cold as each other's.

⚡

I am usually up and out of the door before Francis even has time to stir, however as my alarm bursts to life, the space beside me is empty. The hallway light is on and a golden hue bursts beneath the gap of the door. If I listen hard enough, I can hear him rustling in the kitchen. I stomp to the bathroom a little harder than usual.

He's in his navy dressing gown, earphones plugged and back facing me. My nose wiggles and my mouth salivates spotting the hot, black coffee in the cafetiere. It shifts to repulsion as the scent of eggs and bacon wafts into the air.

'Good morning,' Francis smiles, tossing an eggshell into the compost bin. 'I thought I'd treat you.' I quickly glance at the calendar hanging above the microwave. 'Oh no, it's not an occasion,' he continues, 'Just a normal Wednesday.'

'Francis,' I sigh grabbing my travel mug on the drying rack. 'I can't, I've got to go to work.'

'What's five minutes, ay?'

'Francis...' I pour my coffee.

Scrambling the eggs, he adds a heaped teaspoon of butter to the pan, 'You do enough over-time as it is, Aarush can wait—'

'Francis I said no!' My voice cuts through the room. 'What the hell is going on with you? What *is* this?'

'Kathy!'

The burning coffee spills over my fingers. The liquid rolls down my palms and down my sleeve, staining my skin and jumper. I slam the cafetiere down. The crack in the glass is lost in the sea of Francis's worry as he hurries over asking if

THUNDER ONLY HAPPENS WHEN IT'S RAINING

I'm okay.

'Put your hand under cold water—' His hand finds the arch of my back as if to guide me to the sink. I flinch from his touch,

'Oh, will you just *fuck off!?*'

For a while, nothing is said. The silence is filled by the gushing water hitting the metallic sink. My skin no longer aching, I scrub my sleeve desperately, all the while trying to figure out what to say to Francis. We've never sworn at each other before.

Thank you, but I am not hungry this morning.
When did we become so irreversibly broken?
Could you go out and buy a new cafetiere?

'Look Francis,' I turn, but the kitchen is empty. The frying pan, still full of eggs and bacon, has been taken off the hob. The spilt coffee is still on the countertop, dripping a puddle onto the wooden floor and Francis is gone. I cannot hear the TV in the living room or hear his footsteps treading up the stairs. I dry my hands with a threadbare tea towel before dropping it over the brown liquid on the floor. The off-white cotton absorbs the spilt coffee.

On my way out, I grab a spotted banana from the fruit bowl.

The thing people hate about winter, leaving for work in the dark and then going home in the dark, is something I rather enjoy. In the shadows, with my headlights on, tailing cars probably a little too closely, I am part of a collective rather than my individual failings. It also reminds me of my mother and how she taught me to drive.

Having a mother who worked late shifts at the factory, meant that the skies were always dark and the roads were always a parade of lights when we cruised the streets. Yellow lights flooded the empty pavements. Brake lights dazzled my mother's oval brown eyes as she told me to soften my foot as it lowered to the pedal. Sometimes, on the quiet country road, people would speed past with their full beams on, blinding both of us. In a fit of fury, she would flash the full beamers with my headlights, cursing their existence. I had started learning to drive two weeks before I met Francis. A month later I had a qualified license, a fiancé and no mother.

It's 6:07 when I send my first email of the day. I won't get a reply until 8:00 at the earliest, but I feel good. I'm starting the day productively. Ross will be in shortly, so I reach for the half-eaten yoghurt on my desk. If I try and swallow it, I'll probably throw it back up or choke on it. So instead, I throw the food away in the bin. Ross won't see the bins or anyone for that matter other than the cleaner, but hiding it helps all the same. I do the same with the banana.

The keys in the door rattle and Ross's heavy feet shuffle on the carpet. Like me, Ross isn't needed in the office until much later. It seems he is trying to escape something too, his wife and twin girls I assume.

Five months ago, I pulled into the parking lot and saw his newly purchased Nissan Qashqai parked by the entrance. Ross was supposed to be on paternity leave for another five days. I welcomed him back, and quietly suggested he cut his own key to the office, just in case.

He comes into view, the bags under his eyes are dark and his blond hair is wet in places where he's clearly tried to flatten it with water.

'Good morning,' I eventually say after offering a moment of silence.

'Is it?' he asks, plonking his bag on his desk. 'A *good* morning?' The cynicism makes me smile. 'You know the best thing about twins? When one cries, so does the other.'

At the mention of kids, I avert my eyes. It's only a matter of time until Francis brings up the topic again. It was always part of the package: house, marriage and, of course, kids. Somewhere, in a notebook tucked away in a drawer beneath some old theatre tickets, is a list of baby names we picked on our fourth date. I doubt my withered body could even withstand bearing a child. It's just a waiting game until my cycle stops. Seeing Ross every day puts me off more and more. No matter how many playdates I have been on with my sister and nephew, the look on Ross's face is haunting.

The numbers in the office start dwindling rather quickly as the sun sets early. There is a stillness between the gaps of the desks that Ross disrupts by rolling his chair close to mine as we are the only two left. It's been twelve hours since I first gazed at Ross and his tired face. Throughout the working day, the bags under his eyes have lightened and there is an enthusiasm in his voice as he imitates our boss, who had unknowingly conducted today's meeting with a milk moustache on top of his real moustache.

'You could've told him!' I say, wiping a tear from my lower lashes.

'Me?' Ross jerks, he half spins on his chair before reaching over and poking my bare thigh. 'What about you?' The contact, although quick, hovers between us as his hands are only inches from my skin. I pull my skirt down and recross my legs.

'I'm sorry,' he lifts his hands. 'That was inappropriate.' Not as inappropriate as the thoughts that are beginning to race through my mind.

I remember the first time I had thought of someone else in bed, someone that wasn't an adored celebrity or porn star. Someone that was far too close to home and made me realise there was a crack in the foundation of my marriage. Like all breaks, it started out small but when I found myself asking Francis to take me from behind so I was able to climax at the thought of his golf-buddy, I knew it was worse than I imagined.

But with Ross sitting opposite me, his marble grey eyes staring forcefully into mine, this is more than a thought. This is dangerous. Francis had once been that danger, pulling up outside my parent's house on a motorbike with a mullet and a packet of Marlboro Golds in his pocket. Although we now look back laughing, having transitioned to a car and sensible haircut, all the while gagging at the smell of cigarettes, sometimes I long for the thrill of a ride.

So when Ross stands, I follow suit and do not reject his

advances as he pushes me against the wall with his hard lips on top of mine. Pins and papers clatter to the floor, as my body is pressed against the notice board. For the first time in years, with my heart nearly bursting through my ribcage, I am electric. His tongue finds its way to my neck, one hand tightly wrapped around my waist. He pushes the collar of my shirt with the other and kisses my collarbone.

I catch Ross's reflection in the window. It's dark outside and the orange lights in the office illuminate his broad shoulders. It also highlights a tiny woman beneath him, one that I do not recognise, with thinning copper hair and hollow eye sockets. Clothes hang off her body as if she never learnt how to buy clothes that appropriately fit.

The passion that had set me on fire is immediately replaced with a burning hunger and the only thought that comes to mind is lasagne. The desperate and sudden need for food, for the first time in months, transcends all other needs. I push Ross away. He stumbles back, almost falling. He's muttering an apology, how foolish it was to do such a thing. I don't care. His apology will not satiate the sudden emptiness in my stomach. I tell him not to worry as I reach for my keys on my desk. I'm dashing out, leaving all my unfinished work behind, reminding him to lock up before he leaves. I'm already halfway across the car park before he even has the chance to respond.

I approach the dining room, heels still on and handbag in hand, realising it's been weeks since I last sat down to eat. Francis glances up as if a shadow had momentarily caught his attention, before looking back down at his plate of food. It takes him a moment to realise it is me, hovering under the archway looking in. He blinks at me slowly, lowering his cutlery. Normally by now, I'm halfway up the stairs crying or muttering some lame excuse as to why I can't, or rather won't, eat. Opposite Francis, in a seat that has been cold for far too long, is an empty plate and wine glass. He's laid out the table for me, napkin and all.

'Hi,' he finally says. The corners of his eyes are slightly

red and he's reaching for a crumpled tissue on the table, tucking it into his sleeve. 'Are you okay?'

'Nope,' I shake my head, my lower lip beginning to quiver. 'Are you?'

He waits a moment, swallowing hard, before responding, 'No, not at all.'

Steam from the reheated, half-eaten lasagne sits in the middle of the table.

'Got enough for me?'

He's nodding, on his feet opening the chair for me like he had done on our first date many moons ago. I take my place. As he's dishing up my plate, he apologises,

'Had I known, I would've made something nice.'

'No,' I smile, my stomach rumbling. 'This is perfect.'

STREET LADDER

I always get to the motel before my client, cardinal rule. It ensures that they haven't hidden any sneaky secrets that they can use against me. I enter the empty room, checking crevices I have known clients to hide their sneaky secrets; under the bed is a great place to hide rope; between the bedside table is a fantastic gap where cable ties can be tucked away; a strategically placed pair of handcuffs can hook to the bedpost beneath the mattress. All things that can be used on me when I am least expecting. So I check. I even check the bathroom. It's grotty. The kind where the air is so dank, you believe a yellow nicotine film has coated your pupils, the early onset of cataracts or some glaucoma-shit. The sealant around the edges of the sink is coated in mould. The plug has fine dark hairs sticking out of it. It's disgusting. When the fine hairs start wiggling I realise it is in fact a cockroach. I slam the tap on and drown the fucker down the drain, cursing at the putrid scent now wafting from the hole. Water sprays from the tap and droplets roll down the long ladder in my tights. It stretches from my ankle to my thighs where my previous client had been a little too eager.

There is a timid knock at the door. The knock is so soft I almost think for a moment I've made it up, that is until it happens again.

'Hello?' I yell, approaching the sound. There is no reply. I swing the door open and I am faced with an empty balcony, overlooking the dark car park. It's the squeaking of the trainers that makes me poke my head around. Speeding away is a skinny kid in a baggy t-shirt and very tight jeans. His long, shaggy blond hair swaying by his shoulders.

'Oi! You knocked?'

'Candy?' His voice is as small as his stature. He doesn't look me in the eye as he walks, with his tail in between his legs, back towards the motel room.

'That's me.'

'Can-can I—?' He points over my shoulder as I lean on

the door frame. I let him in, swinging the motel door shut. The noise makes him wince. He's looking around as if the bogeyman is lurking in the shadows. He's far too young.

'So—'

'I.D.' I extend my hand, 'Show me your I.D.'

'I-I am old enough.'

I wiggle my fingers. He pulls out a Velcro wallet and I resist the urge to laugh. I haven't seen a Velcro wallet since the '90s. The driver's licence, belonging to Dominic Ros, says 2002. I start counting from 2002 to 2010 which is—

'2002, so I'm twenty.'

'I know that!' I flick the I.D. at his chest which he clumsily catches. 'Money?'

That Velcro wallet looked far too thin. From his other back pocket, he pulls out a wad of notes, tied in an elastic band. I gesture for him to leave it on the table, which he does. When he's far away enough from both me and the cash, I pick the money up. This little boy wouldn't dare try to swindle me. I count the money all the same.

The bed springs creak as Dominic lowers himself onto the edge. His fingers tapping on his knees.

'So…how does this work?'

A virgin, basically still a kid. I wanna kick him the fuck out, tell him he doesn't need a sex worker at twenty. Instead, I tell him to lie down. I climb on top of him, slowly lowering my body to his, his protruding hip bones dig against mine. My hand slides down his trousers, his pale skin is burning hot. Sweat is building by his hairline, making his blond baby hairs cling to his forehead.

'You need to relax,' I tell him fondling his flaccid cock. The motherfucker then leans forward to kiss me. 'Whoa! No!' I yank my head away, using my free hand to push his head into the pillow beneath him, 'No kissing.' The sweating had been one thing, the kissing another but when I spot tears in his eyes I'm unable to continue.

'Fuck this,' I pull my hand away from his crotch. "Kid, what the hell is this?'

'No, wait, I'm sorry, I'll try harder,' his voice breaks. He's wiping his eyes as if trying to convince me they're dry.

'Look Dominic—'

'Dom, please call me Dom.'

'Dom.' I huff, reaching for my bag and pulling out a packet of cigarettes. 'You look like you're literally about to shit yourself.' I'm lighting my cigarette as he picks at the skin on the edge of his thumb. When he's unable to pull anymore with his nails, he brings the thumb directly to his mouth and rips at the skin with his teeth. This goes on until I finish my cigarette, stubbing it out on the bedside table.

'I gotta do this,' he whispers, 'I need to do this.'

'You do not need to do anything you do not want to do.'

I hear my sister's voice instead of my own. All the times she had told me that no one put me on the streets, that I had walked out the door and put myself there, found a street corner and called it home. I grab the wad of money still left on the table and tell the kid I'm out of here, that the payment is for wasting my goddamn time.

The kid is stupid, I know, but when he jumps up from the bed and wraps his palm around my bicep to tug me back, he must be legally retarded. *Hands, fingers*. I hate them the most. It's as though every man has fire at the ends of their fingertips. The worst kind of hands caress you, they hold the back of your neck or stroke your cheek. So when this kid lays his hand on me to stop me from leaving, I strike him hard across the face. He drops to the ground, cradling his red cheek, still begging me not to go.

'Please! Please don't! My father, he will see you!'

'Father?' My hand is on the doorknob.

'He's the one that hired you!' He's sobbing. 'He said I needed to go through with all this to make it all go away, to cure me!'

I may have dropped out of school at thirteen, or forcibly removed by my mother, but it doesn't take a genius to figure out what the dad's trying to cure. There's word on the street of sick parents forcing kids to fuck prostitutes in order to rewire their brains. Apparently praying the gay away is no longer enough. Sighing, I extend my hand out to him,

'C'mon,' I wiggle my fingers. I help him off the floor, directing him back to the edge of the bed and give him a moment, taking the opportunity to grab another cigarette. I offer him one, surprised when he takes it and places it in between his lips. I expect him to choke on the smoke as I light it, but Dominic breathes easier than he has since he entered the room.

'I'm sorry for...' He gestures to my arm and face '...you know.'

It's the first time I realise how pretty the kid is. Now I know I'm not stealing his innocence, I can appreciate his youthful skin and shining blue eyes.

'I'm sorry too. I'm sorry your father is a piece of shit.'

The softness on his face disappears at the mention of his father. He takes a long and heavy drag on his cigarette before saying,

'He's a good person, he just doesn't understand.'

There are many things I could tell him, like the old age excuse that 'ignorance is generational' is no longer good enough. Ignorance is a choice, not an infliction. I, however, decide to stay silent. The boy knows this, of course he does, but no matter what his father says or does, Dominic will always love and defend him. No one screws you up like a parent does, I would know.

I approach the window that is draped with damp, green curtains. Not wanting to touch it with my hands I kick it to the side so I'm able to overlook the motel carpark.

'You said he was here, which one?'

Dominic doesn't get up, he just mumbles the car make and colour. Of course his father is a BMW driver. It doesn't take long to locate it, parked in the corner by the bushes, under the only lamppost. I hope he has a baseball bat in his footwell. He's a prime target in this area.

'Stay put,' I say grabbing my bag and swinging it over my shoulder.

'Wait, what are you doing?' He's on his feet, his hands

reaching toward me. Normally I would bat them away, but his fingers wiggle as if he was a toddler wanting to be picked up by his mother.

'Trust me.'

'I'm sure there's a saying out there to never trust a woman from the streets.'

At least the kid is smarter than the father.

The wind is bitter and it bites my skin. I wrap my arms around my body in a pathetic attempt to retain any heat. No matter how many years I've slept rough, I could never adjust to the plummeting temperatures. Often or not I think the years of sleeping in wet sleeping bags and blankets have made me more susceptible to colds and lung infections.

I approach the silver BMW and knock on the window of the driver's side. The glass isn't tinted and through it, I see an overweight, white man in his mid-fifties. He looks like he could be one of my clients. I spot the binoculars on his lap and knock on the glass so hard I think I may smash it. He only winds it down a quarter of the way.

'What do'ya want?'

'Another hour.'

'You what?'

I lean my face into the gap and he pushes himself into the chair as if trying to become one with the fabric.

'Honey,' I breathe. 'Your son is giving me the time of my life, I said another hour.'

I push my hand through the gap, palm up. The fat man leans to the passenger side and hauls an envelope out of the glove compartment. He inches to open it, I'm sure to remove some notes. I cough and shake my head. He places the whole envelope in my hand.

'Normally I charge extra for watching,' I point to the binoculars. 'But I draw the line at incest.' Although shadows encapsulate his face, red heat burns his neck and cheeks. He begins to stammer, trying to muster up some lame excuse.

'Go home buddy,' I smack the hood of the car, 'I'll take care of your son.'

STREET LADDER

Better than you ever will.

Dominic does not ask what happened. There is no need, not when I brandish the envelope. I count the notes and then throw a wad of cash in his direction. It lands in his lap.

'Your father owes us both compensation.' He begins to stuff the money in his Velcro wallet. 'And please, for the love of God, buy yourself a new wallet.'

'I had one but it had the Pride flag stitched into it, so my father...' He doesn't finish the sentence. Instead, he grabs the packet of smokes on the bed. 'Do you mind?'

Normally yes, but I let the kid off. If I was him, I'd be doing a hell of a lot worse than smoking cigarettes. I mean, at his age, I *was* doing a hell of a lot worse. My mother has somehow come out of this situation looking like Mother Theresa in comparison to Dominic's father. I perch myself on the wingback chair by the bed.

'Where is she? Your mother?'

'Dead.'

I expected as much, I don't know why I even asked. A cloud of grief hangs over the kid's head like a storm I recognise. The same storm weathered me into... well, this. My finger pokes into the ladder in my tights, then I pull. Before I know it, I'm ripping and clawing at the nylon material. I'm huffing, puffing and swearing until the tights are completely shredded off.

'Better?' Dominic asks staring absent-mindedly at the ripped material.

'Delightful.'

Into a puff of smoke that hovers around his face, Dominic says, 'Sometimes I think about running away.'

'You got somewhere you can go?' God, I sound like his mother.

'I've got an Auntie on my mum's side I've never met down south,' he stubs out his cigarette. 'Pretty sure I can hunt her down on Facebook.'

I want to tell him that people have their own shit to deal

with, that they will turn people away at their door, or delete messages in their inbox from long-lost relatives, but we all need a little bit of hope sometimes.

'Sounds good kiddo.'

Dominic nestles himself into the duvet when the ringtone from my phone bursts to life. I nearly stumble over the ripped tights when I'm syphering through my bag. Delilah's name flashes. I don't accept personal calls around clients, but as my sister's name vibrates in my hand, and the kid is yawning, I trail into the bathroom.

'What d'ya want?' I pull the door behind me. In the background, I hear crying. 'What's happened?' The phone tightens to my ear. 'Is Lizzy okay?'

'She's fine, I just called to tell you there was an incident with mum, she tried breaking in again.' *She's just like herpes.* 'She was tweaking, demanding to see you, I called the police. She's gone.' *Shame she's not dead.* 'It's frightened Liz, she wants to hear your voice. I did think you'd be busy...'

I open the door, peeking through the gap, the kid is asleep. I tell Delilah to pass the phone. Her voice is soft, like a bird singing when she says the word,

'Mummy.'

'Hi baby,' I breathe. 'I heard you had a bit of a scare, but don't you worry, that wicked witch has been taken far away, to *witch* prison.'

She doesn't laugh, 'But Mummy, the same people that took her... they took you.' They had stormed the flat, nearly ten of the pigs, almost rugby tackling me to the ground, reading my rights. All I could hear, amongst their grunts, was Lizzy screaming.

'Baby,' I whisper when she starts crying again. 'Don't cry, it's oka—'

The phone is pulled away from Lizzy and Delilah soothes her. When the phone is spoken into again, my sister's exasperated voice exhales,

'Right, never mind. I'll call you later when she's settled.'

The line cuts off.

STREET LADDER

Mascara clumps on my lower lashes. I spit into my fingers, using my saliva to remove the black smudges down my cheeks. Lizzy's first cry had been the most beautiful sound I'd ever heard. Her voice silenced the room, the doctors and nurses said nothing, and the monitors ceased to beep. Now her cries torment me.

It's nearly 2 a.m. and I'm ready to leave, but when I spot the kid asleep, tucked into a tight ball, I realise there is nowhere to go. I'm unable to utter the word home, a sofa isn't home. Instead, I watch the boy who's crying in his sleep. I use my index finger to wipe a tear. When no more fall, I sit back in the chair. I can't see Lizzy, I'll only make it worse. Delilah comforts her in ways I only dream of. I close my eyes.

I throw myself out of the chair at the first BANG at the door, steadying my blurred vision as Dominic's father yells outside the motel room.

'OPEN UP! DOMINIC GET OUT HERE!'

I'm pushing the kid away, towards the bathroom. He stumbles. I grab his shoulders so we are square, facing each other. His mother must've been so beautiful.

'Are you serious about wanting out?' I ask, gripping him tightly. 'Running away? Starting new?' Dominic nods as the banging on the door intensifies, becoming more violent and more frequent. 'Fine, get in there, hide yourself behind the shower curtain.' I shove him, hoping the boy fears his father more than cockroaches. Then again, they're one of the same. Once the kid has locked himself away, I reach for the door but not until I strip naked.

In the light of the room, he is uglier than I originally thought. There are patches of sweat on his T-shirt that barely contains his swollen belly. It seems he had intended to storm in but at one look at my breasts, he falters in his steps. He looks down before realising my shaved kitty is on show. He looks up to the sky. The sky, to my surprise, is beginning to lighten. Me and the kiddo must've dozed hard, something I never do, not with cash around my clients.

'Where is he?' Spit froths in the corners of his lips.

'Who?'

'Don't play dumb with me *whore*,' he's found his lady balls to look me in the eyes, '*My son.*'

'Oh, him? He's gone, left about two hours ago.'

'What?' he peeks over my shoulder into the empty room. 'You're lying.'

'Must've been when you went on your McDonald's run. He said something about meeting a guy, didn't quite catch the name. Somethin' about goin' to Pulls Mount.'

'Pulls Mount?' The father asks horrified.

Pulls Mount, also known as Pills Mount. A beautiful reserve, two hours north, where young teens go to fuck and do drugs. With the fire that is burning in his eyes, it is clear that Dominic has no other choice than to run. There is no reasoning with a white, middle-aged man and his shitty opinions. He looks over my shoulder one last time, before having the audacity to ask,

'So my son, he...' He points at my kitty. 'He managed to...'

'Fuck me?' I lean forward using the door as support. 'Better than you will ever be able to fuck any woman in your pathetic life, you dirty hog.' I slam the door in his face.

'WHORE!' he screams on the other side. It doesn't bother me. It's the ones who call sex workers names that would spunk their life savings merely just to touch a naked woman.

I'm hugging the kid, bizarre but nice. I find myself tucking the other half of the envelope into his jean pockets.

'No-no.'

I hush him, 'You should have time to go home and pack, Pull Mount is quite the distance. Then go south to contact your aunt.' He nods. 'I've heard the beaches down there are beautiful,' I kiss the top of his head before shoving him out. 'Now go, go before I mug you and take all my money back.'

He's smiling as he opens the door. The morning sun and

pink sky makes its way into the motel room. Birds start singing their morning song as Dominic says,

'Lizzy is very lucky to have you.'

Nosey bugger. I smile, instructing him to leave the door open. He waves goodbye as I stand in the gentle sun rays. I breathe in the fresh morning air before grabbing my bag and the packet of cigarettes still left on the bed. I laugh when I realise there is only one left. The kid smoked me dry. I pop it in my mouth, lighting it, stepping over the ripped tights and leaving the motel room.

ABOUT THE AUTHOR

Krystal Zammit is a dedicated English Teacher who brings her passion for writing into the classroom. With a Master's degree in Creative Writing from Lancaster University, Krystal leads the creative writing club at her school, nurturing the next generation of storytellers. Alongside her teaching responsibilities, Krystal has pursued professional development, completing an NPQ for lead teaching to further enhance her skills in education. Outside of the classroom, Krystal finds inspiration and joy in spending time with her family and friends, who continually support and encourage her creative pursuits.

Printed in Great Britain
by Amazon